"Do you ever give a straight answer?" Brenda asked.

"Not if I can help it." Kyle understood she wanted to know what made him tick, what made him qualified to protect her, what made him who he was.

But he needed her to trust him without knowing the answers. "I'm not going to let anything happen to you. Trust me. I promise."

Her mouth twisted in a wry grimace. "What choice do I have?"

He grinned again. "Now, that's the spirit." He sobered as he approached the next subject, prepared to do battle. "We need to figure out a more secure location for you."

Dark eyebrows shot up almost to her hairline. "Excuse me?"

He gestured toward the covered window. "Too many places a sniper could take a shot from. The outside hallway's too tight. A perfect place for an ambush. If we needed to escape, all anyone would have to do is pick us off as we came out the door."

A visible tremor worked over her. "I don't know where we could go."

"I do."

Books by Terri Reed

Love Inspired Suspense

Love Inspired

TERRI REED

At an early age Terri Reed discovered the wonderful world of fiction and declared she would one day write a book. Now she is fulfilling that dream and enjoys writing for Love Inspired Books. Her second book, *A Sheltering Love,* was a 2006 RITA® Award finalist and a 2005 National Readers' Choice Award finalist. Her book *Strictly Confidential,* book five in the Faith at the Crossroads continuity series, took third place in the 2007 American Christian Fiction Writers Book of the Year Award, and *Her Christmas Protector* took third place in 2008. She is an active member of both Romance Writers of America and American Christian Fiction Writers. She resides in the Pacific Northwest with her college-sweetheart husband, two wonderful children and an array of critters. When not writing, she enjoys spending time with her family and friends, gardening and playing with her dogs.

You can write to Terri at P.O. Box 19555 Portland, OR 97280. Visit her on the web at www.loveinspiredauthors.com, leave comments on her blog, www.ladiesofsuspense.blogspot.com, or email her at terrireed@sterling.net.

THE
DOCTOR'S
DEFENDER

Terri Reed

Love Inspired

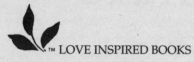

™ LOVE INSPIRED BOOKS

Recycling programs
for this product may
not exist in your area.

ISBN-13: 978-0-373-44508-0

THE DOCTOR'S DEFENDER

Copyright © 2012 by Terri Reed

www.LoveInspiredBooks.com

Printed in U.S.A.

I will say of the Lord, "He is my refuge
and my fortress: my God; in Him I will trust."
—*Psalms* 91:2

To my husband, who is always my hero.

ONE

"You're working late again."

Dr. Brenda Storm glanced up from the open files spread out across her desk and winced. Dr. Sam Johnson walked into her office, looking very *GQ,* with his gelled hair, pressed slacks and starched shirt beneath his white lab coat. She hadn't heard the door open, let alone a knock.

The thought of having to fend off another of his unwelcome advances made her stomach churn. The plastic surgeon might have excellent skills when it came to facial reconstruction, but he hadn't a clue about her lack of interest in him. He was probably so used to women falling at his feet that he saw her disinterest as a challenge.

Well, she wasn't looking for romance. She had too much to accomplish, too much at stake. Her career came first. It would always come first.

And even if she were looking for a relationship, it certainly wouldn't be with some playboy hotshot whose ego was triple his shoe size. She'd made that kind of mistake once when she was young and naive.

She'd fallen for such a guy once her first year of med school. Josh had been cute, smart and charismatic. A total player.

And she'd been just another conquest to brag about.

Humiliated and hurt, she'd vowed then to be more careful when it came to romance. So far her carefulness hadn't lent itself to finding a husband, much to her parents' chagrin.

She forced a smile. "Hi, Sam. What can I do for you?"

His white, even teeth gleamed when he smiled. All practiced charm. It usually worked for him, she was sure, but to her it came across as very phony. Too much like the men her parents were constantly trying to fix her up with. Men who wanted the prestige of having a general surgeon for a wife, but not the lifestyle that went with it.

Long hours and single-minded focus were what got her this far. At thirty-four she was a well-respected general-practice surgeon with ambitions to be department chief. That usually didn't settle well with prospective suitors.

She'd been called a workaholic, too serious, too controlling, too dispassionate...

"Since we're both speaking next Friday, I was thinking maybe we could go together," he said.

She blinked. "Where?"

"The annual fundraiser."

She'd forgotten about the hospital's yearly fall gala. She'd been asked to speak about the technological advances used in general surgery. Ugh. No way of bowing out. She scrambled, searching for a reason why they couldn't "go together" as he put it. "I..."

Gary, the hospital's security guard, poked his head inside the doorway. "Package for you."

Glad for the interruption, she waved him in. In his sixties, the man was twice her age, with graying hair and a wide smile, but he was still strong and capable. He'd been a part of Heritage Hospital long before she'd come aboard. She hoped he'd be around for a long time. He helped out when he saw a need, unlike some of the younger guards who manned the front reception area during various shifts.

Given that Heritage Hospital took up a full block in a very affluent suburb of Chicago, she guessed the younger guards viewed their time at Heritage as a cushy job since they saw little criminal activity on a daily basis. Still, having a security presence gave patients and staff of the hospital a measure of comfort.

And for the doctors and nurses, an extra pair of hands was an extra pair of hands. Welcome when needed.

"These smell delicious." Gary carried a pink bakery box. The distinctive label on the side was from a posh cupcake shop not far from the hospital. "There's a card taped to the top."

Brenda rose and came around the desk to peel the envelope from the top of the box. Inside was a pretty thank-you card. The signature of the sender was illegible. She had no idea who was thanking her or why.

"You get cupcakes from patients?" Sam asked, peering over her shoulder. "All I get are pictures once they've healed. I'd prefer cupcakes."

Brenda received other gifts and tokens of gratitude from patients, nice gestures for doing the job she'd spent her whole life training for. She had more wins than losses. Still, the Hanson case hanging over her head robbed her of appreciating this small thank-you.

Three months ago, Peter Hanson had died on her operating table. He'd come into Heritage Hospital with acute appendicitis. She'd been the surgeon on call and quickly assessed he needed surgery. Everything went smoothly until his heart stopped in the middle of what she'd considered a textbook procedure.

The autopsy had been inconclusive. There had been no heart disease. No blockage. No aortic stenosis, no myocarditis. No genetic issues. No structural damage.

And now his family was suing her and the hospital for malpractice.

A blemish on her otherwise spotless record. She felt sick thinking about it. Had she done something wrong, made some crucial mistake? The possibilities gnawed at her, eating away at her confidence.

She set the pink bakery box on the desk and opened the lid to reveal four fancy cupcakes with colorful sprinkles atop fluffy white frosting and little smiley-faced rings, the kind usually meant for children.

Brenda normally didn't operate on children. At least not at Heritage Hospital. However, she did treat patients of all age ranges and walks of life at the downtown clinic she'd helped establish.

In the past couple of years, she'd taken out an inflamed appendix on a ten-year-old girl, adenoids for a preteen boy, a ruptured spleen on a six-year-old and tonsils from at least three prepubescent kids. Had this come from one of those families? Or had these been the only available cupcakes at the bakery? That seemed more likely.

"Yum. Those are from Blissful Indulgence," Sam said. "So much goodness in a small package."

The cupcakes didn't look that small to Brenda. Each confection looked to have about five hundred grams of fat ready to clog arteries. "Help yourselves."

"Don't mind if I do," Gary said and reached to take a cupcake. He peeled back the paper wrapper around the bottom and took a bite. After he swallowed, he said, "Thanks, Dr. Storm. These are amazing." He left the office with a smile.

Sam picked up a cupcake but didn't take a bite. "You still haven't answered my question. The fall gala? Us going together?" He gave her a searching look. "Unless, of course, you already have a date."

No date. And she didn't want one with him. Or anyone for that matter. "Let me think about it and get back to you."

"I know what that means," Sam replied with a slightly petulant tone.

Maybe he had more of a clue than she'd thought. She'd give him an A for persistence.

Gary reappeared at the door. "Help," he croaked, clinging to the door frame, his face ashen as he slid to the floor in a heap.

Alarm jolted through Brenda. Heart attack? A massive coronary, perhaps.

She pushed Sam out of the way and ran to Gary. She rolled him over. "Call for help."

"On it." Sam picked up the phone on the desk.

She placed her fingers against Gary's neck, hoping to find a carotid pulse. He had none. Her stomach sank. "No pulse. Not breathing."

Sam spoke into the phone. "Code Ninety-nine. Dr. Storm's office."

Dread chipped away at her composure. She tilted Gary's head back and tugged his jaw forward to open the airway. From her coat pocket, she grabbed a microshield CPR mask and placed it over his lips, fitting the mask air valve against his tongue. The faint scent of almonds wafted from his mouth. "Beginning CPR."

* * *

"Gary died from cyanide poisoning?" Stunned, Brenda sat back in the armchair across the expansive mahogany desk from Ned Landsem, Heritage Hospital's administrator. Her stomach roiled at the news. The smell of almonds on Gary's breath hadn't come from the flavoring in the cupcakes but from poison.

Despite her and the staff's best efforts, Gary had died. Her heart ached at the loss. She tucked her sadness away in the deep depths of her heart. Compartmentalizing came with the job. "How? Why?"

"I don't have all the details." Nearer to seventy than sixty, Ned Landsem was still a dashing man with thick white hair and a robust personality that made working for him a joy. "The police suspect the cupcakes that were delivered to you were laced with cyanide. Once toxicology comes back, they'll have confirmation."

Realization slammed into her like a gale-force wind coming off Lake Michigan in the winter. Someone had tried to kill her. Shock stole the breath from her lungs.

She shuddered as anxiety and fear dug deep talons through her, leaving weeping wounds. Someone wanted her dead.

And had murdered Gary instead.

Tears burned the backs of her eyes. A senseless death.

"The police don't have the resources to give you round-the-clock security, so the hospital has hired a protection specialist from Trent Associates."

She drew back. "'Protection Specialist,' as in bodyguard?"

"We had to move quickly. Trent Associates has an exemplary reputation. They were able to send someone out right away."

She sat forward. "I don't get a say in this?"

Though she logically understood the need for a bodyguard and could see the value, she hated not being in control of her own destiny. And having someone out there who wanted her dead made her feel vulnerable in a way she'd never felt before. She didn't like it one bit.

His expression turned parental. "You're an important member of our staff, Brenda. Your safety is our priority. We care about you."

As good as the sentiment felt, she had no illusions about her worth. Her skills in the operating room made her a high-priced commodity, one other hospitals and private practices sought after.

But on a personal level, she wasn't that close to the staff. Relationships only complicated matters. It was easier to keep people at a distance than to risk disappointment. Theirs and hers.

"I'm sure the staff would appreciate the extra security." The weight of responsibility pressed on her shoulders. Someone had already been hurt because of her; the least she could do was accept the hospital's generous gesture.

Ned nodded his approval. "I'm glad you understand. This will be in everyone's best interest—"

A knock interrupted him. "Come in."

The door to the office opened. She looked over her shoulder to see the newcomer. Her breath stalled out.

Ned rose and came around the desk, his hand outstretched. "Mr. Martin, I trust your trip went well."

A tall, lean and drop-dead gorgeous man strode forward and halted beside her chair. He wore khaki cargo pants and a loose-fitting shirt more appropriate for a pool party than a professional meeting. And he wore flip-flops on his feet. Did he plan to head to the lake-shore when he was done here?

"Yes, without a hitch. You must be Dr. Landsem." The two men shook hands.

Surely this wasn't her bodyguard. Brenda frowned in confusion. Weren't bodyguards supposed to look tough and intimidating? Like James Bond or something?

This guy with his shaggy blond hair belonged on a movie set for a beach flick or a photo shoot for a male hottie-of-the-month calendar. Not that she didn't appreciate his handsomeness. She was a woman with a pulse. She rather liked his angular jawline and full lips.

Lively sky-blue eyes met hers. His gaze slowly raked over her in silent appraisal. Would he see the flaws she worked hard to hide?

The corners of his mouth lifted in a smile as if pleased with what he saw. Her pulse skyrocketed.

She sat up straighter. Oh, no. No, no, no. This guy couldn't be the protection specialist the hospital hired. He was too…too much. Too young. Too good-looking. Not a man to be easily ignored.

Ned gestured to the man and said, "Dr. Brenda Storm, I'd like you to meet Kyle Martin. Your body-guard."

"Hi there, Dr. Storm, I've heard good things about you." Kyle Martin extended his hand toward the brunette beauty sitting perfectly straight in the leather arm-chair.

She didn't move. Her lips pressed into a firm line. She couldn't disapprove of him already, could she? No matter, she wouldn't be the last.

Odd that she'd wear all black beneath her white lab coat on a hot late-September day. Black slacks, black buttoned-up blouse. Okay, not everything was black. Her red pumps sporting little embroidered roses were in vivid contrast to the stark outfit. Not as somber as she wanted others to believe? Interesting. And intriguing.

Her dark hair was twisted up in a fancy bun in the back. He wondered what she'd do if he undid the pins holding her hair. She'd look softer with all that mass spilling about her shoulders.

Probably slug him. His lips twitched with a suppressed chuckle.

"Okay, we'll skip the pleasantries," he said. "I hear you've had a tough time lately." He'd read the dossier on her during the plane ride from Boston. A lot of facts but no real hint of her personality.

She slanted him a glance. Were those tears shimmering in her dark eyes? "If you mean someone trying to poison me and instead killing a sweet man who'd done nothing wrong except indulge in a pretty cupcake, then yeah, I'd say a tough time."

She was not impressed. Tough. Like it or not, she was stuck with him.

"And being sued for malpractice. I'd say that qualifies, as well."

With a quick glance at her boss, she said, "Well, you can hardly protect me from that, now can you?"

"You'd be surprised what I can do," Kyle quipped.

She jumped to her feet, her dark eyes no longer filled with tears. Now they flashed with indignation. "I do not need you."

Kyle grinned. "Yes, you do need me. I'll be sticking to you like surf wax to a surfboard until the police catch the person who tried to harm you. No one's getting near you without going through me."

Her eyes widened. Her mouth clamped shut. She

swung her gaze to the boss man. "This won't work. I can't have him—" she waved a hand in Kyle's direction "—with me in the O.R. The man has on flip-flops. Please, Ned. This isn't a good idea."

"It's an excellent idea." Ned tipped his chin in Kyle's direction. "Mr. Martin will take very good care of you."

"I don't need to be taken care of," she argued. "I need to get back to work."

Ned slipped an arm around her shoulders. "Once the police find who tried to hurt you, everything should all settle down."

"If it doesn't, then what?" she asked with a quick glance toward Kyle.

Kyle widened his grin, enjoying the myriad emotions traipsing across her expressive face. She'd bounced from sorrow, to fear, to anger to more anger in the space of a heartbeat.

Her frown deepened.

Okay, shadowing the doctor for the next few days was going to be a challenge. But man, she was easy on the eyes. That was a huge plus. Not that it mattered what she looked like. Protection was protection. He'd do his job and then walk away like always. That was why he liked his job. Each assignment was different, mostly interesting and always temporary.

He was a temporary type of guy.

Especially when it came to women. Prickly women, like the doctor, in particular.

"All we can do is pray the police find whoever did this and arrests them quickly," Ned said.

"What if they don't?" she asked, her voice rising slightly.

Clearly, she was more freaked out by the threat hanging over her head than she'd like to admit. Kyle figured the doctor was used to being in charge and having everything under control. Most doctors he knew did.

But this was a situation she couldn't control. He'd have to pick his battles. He didn't need to be distracted by fighting her for control when a very real and dangerous threat loomed on the horizon. Who knew when this nut job would strike again?

"The police department is top-notch. They'll find the suspect soon," Kyle said, hoping to alleviate her stress.

Fear marched across her pretty face. "Fine. You can protect me." Her voice hitched on the last word. She glanced at the thin gold watch on her delicate wrist. "I'm due in the O.R. in ten." She gestured to his feet. "Do you have other shoes?"

He grinned and gave her a mock salute. "Yes, ma'am."

Her lips thinned as she turned away and stepped toward the door. "Just stay out of my way."

Kyle snagged her wrist. His palm came in contact with her bare skin, soft and smooth. Her pulse jumped beneath his fingers. Kyle couldn't figure out what he'd done to upset her. It usually took longer before he offended someone.

"I promise this won't be so bad," he said, his voice coming out huskier than he liked. "You'll hardly even know I'm around."

She arched a raven-black eyebrow but didn't shy away from his touch. "That'll be a feat."

Not sure what to make of her remark, he shrugged and let go of her. "I can be unobtrusive."

"We'll see." She shimmied past him and exited the room.

Ned clapped Kyle on the back. "You have your work cut out for you. But I trust you'll keep her safe."

His gaze remained on the door. "On my life."

He only hoped the prickly doctor let him do his job.

Five hours later, exhausted from the stress of her bodyguard's watchful eye during two minor surgeries, Brenda led the way to her condo. They took the elevator to the fifteenth floor. Her stomach fluttered with nerves. The space was too confining. He was too close. She was having way too much trouble ignoring the waves of attraction sizzling between them. She met his gaze in the reflection off the smooth metal doors. He seemed to see right through her, to her very core.

She averted her gaze, mad at herself for the ridiculous thought.

Just how was this going to play out? Surely he wasn't expecting to sleep in her apartment. She could only pray he'd make sure she was safely inside and then disappear until morning.

Wishful thinking.

As she approached her door, she dug inside the bag slung over her shoulder and pulled out a set of keys. She reached to insert the key in the doorknob. As quick as lightning, her new bodyguard snaked an arm around her waist and hauled her backward, against his hard chest. Awareness of his muscles and strength slipped over her like a sheet of silk.

Maybe she'd been wrong to think this man couldn't be tough and intimidating.

"What are you doing?" she demanded, trying to reconcile the warmth spreading through her to the outrage she should be feeling at being manhandled so unceremoniously. She couldn't quite get there though.

His corded arm and the musky scent of his aftershave distracted her. Not to mention the fact that she hadn't had this kind of close contact with a man in… well, a long time.

"Saving you from yourself." His whispered answer tickled her ear and caused a rippling effect of shivers to course through her. "The door could be booby-trapped. Someone wants you dead, remember?"

If he was trying to frighten her, he succeeded. Her stomach rolled. She hated how vulnerable she felt. Someone out there wanted to hurt her and didn't care who they hurt in the process. And she didn't know who or why. She could only guess and make assumptions. She bit her lip, a habit she'd dropped years ago but fear had resurrected.

Kyle set her aside. Impossibly she felt even more vulnerable without his strong arms around her. He moved closer to the door and slowly ran his hand around the edges of the frame, inspected the lock and then held out his hand. "Keys?"

She handed over her flashlight key chain with all her keys. "The silver, square one."

He inserted the key in the lock and turned it. Brenda winced, half expecting an explosion. None came. He turned the handle and cracked the door, once again inspecting the edges.

"What are you looking for?" she asked, grimacing at how small her voice sounded.

"Trip wires." He pushed the door wide. "Door's not rigged." He held up a hand. "Let me clear the place first."

She blinked with alarm as he withdrew a gun he'd kept hidden at his back beneath the loose shirt. Now she better understood his garb. He dressed to conceal his weapon.

Probably made people underestimate him, just as

she'd done when she'd first set eyes on him. He entered the condo with the gun held in front of him and disappeared from view while she waited in the hallway. Her gaze strayed to the elevators, half expecting some bogeyman to come bounding out.

Kyle returned, the gun out of sight and a grin on his handsome face. "Nice place."

"Thanks," she said automatically.

Though the idea of him entering her home and inspecting every nook and cranny left her feeling exposed. She never let anyone into her inner sanctum. But she didn't have a choice. And that grated on her. Her unknown assassin had taken her options away. Anger stirred, mixing with the fear.

She placed her purse on the maple side table just inside the doorway. Since she'd worked a double shift at the hospital and had stayed the night there last night, the place smelled musty and hot after several days of being closed up.

She went straight to the window, drew back the floor-to-ceiling drapes and cracked the windows to let in some fresh air. They were fifteen floors up with an unobstructed view of Lake Michigan. The sight of sailboats gliding on the blue water made her smile. She wished she were out there, where the only thing she had to worry about was the wind and the rigging.

"This view is the reason I picked this building," she explained. "I'm a little farther from the hospital than I'd prefer, but being this close to the lake and having this view makes the trek worth it."

"Fantastic view, but a security nightmare," Kyle commented as he moved to stand directly in front of her. He propelled her back several feet.

She cocked her head. "How can you say that? No building lines up directly with this one."

"A sniper doesn't need a direct angle." He rocked back on the heels of the loafers he'd changed into earlier. "I could make the shot from the roof of the structure to the right, no sweat."

She peered over his shoulder to the rooftop of the closest apartment building. Chills swept over her despite the humidity. Great. Now she had to worry about snipers, too.

He drew the drapes closed, shrouding them in a false sense of intimacy.

"I'm starved." Kyle flashed a breath-stealing grin.

She didn't know if she'd get used to that. He'd been a constant distraction all day. She'd had to force herself not to glance at him during her surgeries for fear she'd make a mistake and slice where she shouldn't.

She normally didn't have a problem concentrating while performing an operation. In fact her single-minded focus set her apart from other doctors who liked to talk or listen to music during a procedure. Not her. She needed the room quiet so the patient had her complete attention.

But today…though Kyle had remained quiet and out of the way near the door as promised, he might as well have been wearing a neon flashing light. The man disturbed her on so many levels.

"We can order in or there's a good Thai place around the corner," she said, glad for the neutral subject.

"Thai sounds good. Plus, we can talk about how this is going to work. Set some ground rules."

"Rules?"

His grin widened. "Yep."

Her stomach clenched.

Needing some space, she said, "I'll change and we can go eat." And talk about the rules. Oh, joy.

She retreated to the sanctuary of her bedroom and closed the door, grateful for the momentary respite from his overwhelming presence. There was something about him, his energy and charisma, that made the air around him vibrate. It was exhausting. And thrilling.

She quickly changed out of her hospital attire and into casual clothes. She hesitated before stepping out of her room. How was she going to survive the next few days with that hunk of a man in the other room dogging her every step? Physical distance from him wasn't possible. He was here to protect her, and that meant sticking close. But she could keep an emotional distance. She was good at that.

Kyle studied the professional portrait hanging over the gas fireplace in Brenda's living room. The image captured a very stern-looking man—who Kyle guessed was Brenda's father—a perfectly coiffed dark-haired woman—presumably Mrs. Storm—and Brenda as a young woman. Probably late teens, Kyle decided.

Her raven hair was gathered to one side by a thin ribbon, her face fuller, her smile uncomfortable, as if she'd posed for far too long and wanted to escape. Brenda resembled both parents in various ways. She had her mother's brunette hair, her father's slim nose. The shape of her eyes was more her father's, while the color was a tad darker than her mother's.

He wondered what it had been like growing up with two parents. Two parents who cared.

He shook his head to dispel that mistruth. His mother had cared before she'd died. His father...not so much.

Thoughts of his past had no place in this assignment.

He turned from the portrait and moved to look at more framed photos gracing the cream-colored wall leading to the hallway. Each photo was posed, with perfect lighting and perfect expressions. Not one candid shot among the lot.

In fact, he couldn't remember seeing anything in the apartment during his security check that wasn't perfectly arranged, perfectly ordered.

Very little to suggest someone actually lived here.

His gaze made a slow sweep over the condo. Except for her purse sitting on the little stand by the door, there was nothing personal in view. The place reminded him of a hotel suite.

Something was off here. From all accounts, Dr. Brenda Storm was a highly skilled surgeon sought after by the best hospitals in the world. She was paid well for her work and had prestige most would envy. Yet, she lived like a guest in her own home.

A door down the hall opened and Brenda emerged from her bedroom. She'd changed from the austere black outfit, which she'd put back on after discarding her operating scrubs, to a fitted navy skirt that showed off her curves admirably and white sleeveless blouse that made her look delicate. Her idea of casual?

A knock sounded on the door.

Kyle stilled, his senses at attention. "Expecting someone?"

Brenda shook her head, her eyes growing round. "No."

Kyle motioned her back toward the kitchen. He approached the door from the side and peered through the peephole. An array of pink and purple flowers blocked the view. Whoever was on the other side of the door was holding a bouquet of flowers in front of his or her face.

"Know of anyone who would send you flowers?" he asked.

"No one."

Kyle withdrew his gun.

Time to meet this threat head-on.

TWO

Kyle pressed his back against the inside wall next to Brenda's front door. Nerves stretched tight, he regulated his breathing. Brenda's life was at stake here. He needed to keep control of the situation. "What do you want?"

"Floral delivery," came the muffled reply. "For Dr. Brenda Storm. Is she here?"

Wariness narrowed Kyle's focus. She didn't need to be home for the flowers to be delivered. He could have left them at the front desk. How had the guy slipped past the doorman?

Brenda moved forward. "Who—"

Kyle lifted a finger to keep her quiet. He waved her back again. She nodded and stepped closer to the kitchen archway. "She's not available. Take them back."

"I can't. I've got a schedule to keep. My boss will have my head if I return to the shop without delivering them. Guy paid to have them delivered pronto."

"Guy?" Kyle wasn't sure he bought the story. "You have the name of who sent them?"

"Yeah."

A heartbeat of silence passed. "Well, what's it say?"

"You gonna open the door, or what?"

"No, you're gonna tell me through it."

"My hands are kinda full here, in case you hadn't noticed."

Obviously, he knew Kyle was watching through the peephole. If he were an assailant, he knew he wasn't going to have an easy time of it today. "Leave the flowers on the floor and back up ten steps."

Kyle watched through the peephole. The flowers were lowered. A man wearing a black fedora perched low over gray eyes stepped back. He was older than Kyle would have thought, given the job. He wore jeans and a T-shirt, making an odd contrast with his hat. He held a clipboard and flowers.

"I said flowers on the ground," Kyle repeated.

The vase of the flowers lowered to the floor.

Cautiously, Kyle opened the front door, careful to keep his weapon at the ready yet out of sight. One wrong move...

The delivery guy moved closer.

Kyle countered with a step forward, drawing on the guy.

"Whoa! Dude!" He raised his hands in the air. Fear widened the man's gray eyes. "I need your John Hancock on the last line." He lowered the clipboard slightly.

"Keep your hands where I can see them." Kyle grabbed the clipboard and inspected the form. It looked legit. So did the flowers. The name of the flower shop was emblazoned across the top of the form.

"How long have you worked for this store?" Kyle asked.

The guy swallowed. "A few weeks. I'm lucky to have a job in this economy."

True enough statement. The state of the job market had hit everyone hard. Kyle signed for delivery. "So who sent them?"

The guy shrugged and gestured with his chin to the vase. "There's a card." He tried to peer over Kyle's shoulder. "Is the doctor home?"

Shoving the clipboard into the guy's chest and pushing him back another step, Kyle replied, "She's not available."

"You her boyfriend?"

Kyle narrowed his gaze on the man. "Time for you to go."

The guy held up his hands. "Hey, man, just asking. Didn't mean anything by it." He retreated, going down the hall to the elevator, then disappearing inside.

Kyle stared down at the array of bright flowers. A small white envelope peeked out among the blooms. Squatting down, he inspected the water-filled, fluted clear vase. He scrutinized the blossoms, looking for anything suspicious. There didn't seem to be any substance coating the petals. He didn't see any hidden items that would suggest the flowers had been tampered with. He carefully ran a finger around the rim of the vase to check for wires or anything that would indicate the bouquet was rigged with an explosive device.

When he was satisfied that the arrangement wasn't fitted to detonate, he lifted the vase and carried it inside the condo. Brenda stood stock-still in her kitchen, her hands gripping the marble counter, her knuckles white.

Her upset had his insides knotting. He wanted to ease her fears. "It's okay. Guy's gone." He set the vase on the counter. "Nothing dangerous here but flowers."

Wariness crossed her face. She backed away. "Who sent them?"

"There's a note card," he said. "Do you have a plastic baggie?"

She opened a drawer. Inside were neatly placed boxes of plastic bags. "Which size?"

"Sandwich."

She withdrew one and handed it over. He tore off a paper towel from the dispenser near the sink and used the sheet to protect the tall plastic cardholder from his fingerprints as he lifted the thing from the flowers and set it on the counter. He'd worked long enough with several ex–law enforcement personnel to know how to be cautious and preserve possible evidence. Still using the paper towel, he removed the envelope from the prongs and flipped up the seal.

He slid the card-stock note out and read the scrawling words out loud. "Hope your day will be better now. Are we on for next Friday? It's signed Sam."

A frown pinched the space between Brenda's winged eyebrows. "A doctor at the hospital."

"Your boyfriend?" From the dossier he'd read on her, she wasn't married, engaged or involved in a serious relationship that they knew of. But that didn't mean there wasn't someone in her life. Kyle didn't understand why the thought bothered him. Of course Brenda had to be seeing someone. A looker like her couldn't be unattached. She probably had a dozen men clamoring for her attention.

She gave a vehement shake of her head. "No. Not even close. He's too...not my type."

Now why did that please him? And just what was her type? Not that the type of man she dated mattered. His job wasn't to pass judgment or probe his protectee's psyche. Though if they'd met under different circumstances... He gave himself a mental shake. Not. Going. There. "This Sam would like to date you, though."

She sighed. "He's asked. Often. Wants me to go to

the hospital fundraising gala with him next Friday. He can't seem to get it through his brilliant thick skull that I'm not interested."

"The gala is out." No way would he let her go anywhere near such a security risk.

She frowned. "I have to be there."

He shook his head. "No, you don't. Your boss will understand."

Her lips pressed into a firm line. A sign of acquiescence? He doubted it. But that was a battle they could have at a later date.

To preserve the note, he slipped it into the baggie and then placed it into his shirt pocket. "What's this doctor's full name?"

"Samuel Johnson."

"I'll have a background check run on him."

She drew back slightly. "Sam would never hurt me."

"Maybe the doctor has someone in his life who'd like to get rid of the competition. I need to know the players in this game."

"Game? This isn't a game! This is my life!"

The outrage and fear in her face twisted him up inside. He held out a hand, palm facing out. "Sorry, didn't mean anything by that. Just a figure of speech. You're right, this isn't a game. I take it very seriously."

Her lovely features turned stony. She went into the living room and sat on a plush chair. "I hate this. Hate feeling scared and out of control."

He followed her and squatted beside her. "That's understandable. And you're doing great."

"Yeah, we'll see how I'm doing by the time this is done." She scoffed and shook her head. "I can't imagine living in fear for very long. Always wondering if the next knock at the door might be a deranged killer.

Who knows what else this crazy person will try. Or who might get hurt because of me."

"That's why you have me. I'll protect you. You might not believe it, but I'm very good at what I do."

Her dark eyes searched his face. "Why do you do this? Work as a bodyguard, I mean?"

Uncomfortable with the focus turning to him, he rose. And deflected. He was good at deflecting. "Guy's got to make a living."

"There are other ways to make a living." The studied way she peered at him made him think of microscopes and petri dishes. He wasn't some bacterium she had to try to understand. "Less dangerous ways."

A shudder worked its way through him. "Yeah, boring ways."

He had no doubt that, being a surgeon, she saw the aftermath of dangerous careers and hobbies alike, which gave her a different perspective. She could never understand the inherent need to live life on the edge, to push as close to danger as possible, to risk life and limb to feel alive, to feel…something.

"Ah, you're a thrill seeker, then." There was just the barest hint of censure in her tone.

He grinned, undaunted by the disapproval. It wasn't the first time a woman said that to him. It wouldn't be the last. "Always looking for the next gnarly wave to come rolling in."

"Gnarly, huh? You're a surfer?"

"That obvious?"

A slight smile played at the corners of her mouth. He had the sudden longing to see a full-blown smile, to hear her laugh, to see her relax. So not what he should be concentrating on. Her physical well-being was his priority. Not her mental health.

"Yes, it is," she admitted. "But I can't imagine there's much surfing in Boston. You must not have grown up there."

"No, I didn't. Southern Cal. On some of the best beaches in the world."

A momentary bout of nostalgia hit. He missed the California sunshine and the smell of the Pacific Ocean. The Atlantic smelled different. Brinier. "There's always windsurfing in Massachusetts. You can be at a great surf spot within two hours from downtown Boston."

He remembered the last time he'd been out on the Atlantic Ocean planing across the tips of the waves, catching enough speed to loop. "Not quite the same rush as traditional surfing...but still fun."

"How did you end up in Boston?"

She was full of questions, and that wasn't a tale he cared to share. Revealing his painful past wasn't part of his job description. He kept his life under wraps. Better that way. He'd hate to see the look of pity or judgment or both in pretty Brenda's eyes if she knew how he'd ended up where he was. "Life. Funny how it works out sometimes."

"Did you move there because of a wife or girlfriend?"

He arched an eyebrow. She was fishing to see if he was attached. Interesting. "No wife, no girlfriend."

"Why not?"

"I could ask you the same thing," he shot back.

She hesitated. "I've been focused on my career."

"Ah. But someday you hope to get married?" He wondered what kind of man would snag the doctor's heart.

"Don't you?" she countered without answering his question.

"No," he stated with certainty.

She studied him. "Why not?"

He thought about that for a moment. He wasn't sure where his reluctance to relationships stemmed from. Maybe it was his parents' rocky marriage before his mother's death. Or maybe the way his high-school girl-friend, Anne Tucker, had stomped all over his heart when she'd gone to the prom with his best friend be-cause Kyle hadn't the money to pay for their ticket. She'd ended up pregnant that night. Kyle knew he'd dodged a bullet, or rather a situation that he wouldn't have been able to handle. A kid at seventeen? No way.

Better not to get too involved with any woman and avoid such a sticky and permanent situation.

Realizing the doc was waiting for an answer, he went with the easy one. The one he knew would keep her at arm's length. "I like playing the field. Keeping my op-tions open."

She stiffened. The corners of her mouth tightened. "What training do you have? How do I know my life is safe in your hands?"

Appeasing her curiosity and reassuring her he could protect her were two different things. He held his right hand up, his index and middle fingers in a V shape. "Cub Scout promise. I had my Bobcat pin within the first three months. Had it turned right side up by the next day."

Irritation crossed her face. "I have no idea what that means."

"You wouldn't. You're a girl. Only boys can be Cub Scouts."

She rolled her eyes. "Do you ever give a straight answer?"

"Not if I can help it." He understood she wanted to know what made him tick, what made him qualified to protect her, what made him who he was. That was only natural. But he needed her to trust him without knowing the answers. "I'm not going to let anything happen to you. Trust me." He made the Cub Scout sign again. "I promise."

Her mouth twisted in a wry grimace. "What choice do I have?"

He grinned again. "Now that's the spirit." He sobered as he approached the next subject, prepared to do battle. "We need to figure out a more secure location for you."

Dark eyebrows shot up almost to her hairline. "Excuse me?"

He knew that wouldn't go over well. He gestured toward the covered window. "Too many places a sniper could take a shot from. The outside hallway's too tight. A perfect place for an ambush. If we needed to escape, all anyone would have to do is pick us off as we came out the door."

A visible tremor worked over her. "I don't know where we could go."

"The dossier said your parents have a home in Forest Park. The house is armed with a state-of-the-art alarm system."

She shook her head. "I would hate to put them in danger."

"It will be safer there."

"I don't know…"

He'd hoped to ease into this over Thai food. "It's already been arranged."

Her eyes widened with outrage. "You've spoken to my parents?"

"Trent is thorough in our protection."

She made a face. "Unbelievable."

"We've been here long enough. Do you want to pack a few things?"

"What choice do I have?" Anger laced her words.

Empathy twisted his stomach in knots. He knew firsthand how upsetting, annoying and humiliating it was to have someone else calling the shots. "It's for your safety."

"Of course it is." Though the words dripped with sarcasm, her posture was resigned. She returned to her room. A few minutes later she came out carrying a small suitcase. "I have some clothes already at their house."

"Do you want to keep the flowers?" he asked.

She shook her head. "No. Let's leave them in the lobby."

He wondered briefly if it was the flowers themselves or the sender she wanted to leave behind.

He escorted her to his rental car, a black Suburban. The modern, everyday version of the layman's tank. He did a quick sweep of the exterior before allowing her too close to the vehicle. Checked the undercarriage, made sure the doors hadn't been tampered with. Standard operating procedure. When he was sure the SUV was safe, he helped Brenda into the passenger seat.

As he drove he kept a vigilant eye out for a tail. Nothing. A half hour later they arrived at her parents' Forest Park home. Behind a gated community, which provided twenty-four-hour security, the Storms' residence was a large, gabled brick house with manicured hedges, Astroturf green lawns and flower beds with a kaleidoscope of colorful flora and visually interesting plants. A magazine-worthy home.

"Nice place," Kyle commented. A far cry from the

double-wide prefabricated place he'd called home as a kid. "You grew up in this house?"

"No. My parents bought this home after I'd graduated from med school."

"Where did you live as a kid?"

She opened the passenger door. "Evanston."

"Did you go to Northwestern?"

"I did. The university was practically in my backyard." She climbed out of the vehicle and walked toward the house.

Kyle grabbed her suitcase from the back and followed her to the front door. Humidity made his shirt stick to his back. He glanced around, noting the quiet street and the other homes visible over the hedges marking the property lines. The hedges weren't exactly the best for security—too many places a bad guy could slip through undetected.

He would have preferred a fence or a rock wall. Better yet, barbed wire.

Brenda opened the door. "Mom, Dad, I'm home."

The temperature change between the outside and the inside was drastic. The sweat from the late-September humidity outside chilled on Kyle's skin. Brenda rubbed her arms as goose pimples appeared.

As they stepped around the entryway corner, a well-dressed woman hastily shoved amber pill bottles into the drawer of the side table. A gray-haired man lay stretched out in a recliner. He adjusted the blanket covering him over his torso and legs. If he was cold, why not turn down the air conditioner? The place was like a meat locker.

"You're here early," her mother said, her voice sounding strained. Her red eyes made Kyle think she'd been crying recently. No doubt upset by Brenda's brush with death.

The photos in Brenda's apartment didn't do Mrs. Storm justice. Kyle could see the resemblance between mother and daughter. Mrs. Storm's dark hair was cut short to frame her youthful face. If not for the silver streaks, Kyle wouldn't have guessed she was old enough to be Brenda's mother. "We weren't expecting you until later this evening. Are you all right?" Mrs. Storm asked.

"I'm fine, Mom." Brenda went to her father's side and pressed a hand to his forehead. "Dad, are you okay? You look feverish."

Mr. Storm shooed her away. His eyes were not quite focused. "Stop your fussing. You're not my doctor."

"Just a cold, dear," Mrs. Storm said quickly, though she wouldn't meet her daughter's gaze. "You know your father. Nothing for you to fret about."

Kyle's chest knotted at the hurt in Brenda's pretty eyes as she stepped back.

"Brenda, please introduce your guest," Mrs. Storm said.

"Mom, Dad, this is Kyle Martin of Trent Associates, the bodyguard the hospital hired," Brenda said.

"We're so thankful you'll be protecting our daughter." Mrs. Storm offered a smile.

"I will do my best, ma'am," Kyle replied.

"Please call me Maggie."

Mr. Storm held out a hand to Kyle. The effort seemed to cost him energy. Sweat beaded his forehead. "Mr. Martin."

Kyle grasped the older man's hand, noting how thin and fragile the bones felt. The man's grip was stronger than Kyle would have thought given how ill he appeared. "Mr. Storm, it's a pleasure to meet you."

"Ned tells me you come highly recommended." Mr. Storm's gaze focused on Kyle. "Tell me what qualities you to protect my only child."

The man asked virtually the same questions as his daughter. "Ex–special operations, Navy."

Releasing his hand, Mr. Storm gave an approving nod. "Excellent."

One glance at Brenda told Kyle she wasn't as appeased. He'd have some explaining to do. Came with the territory. "Glad we got that settled," Kyle said. "I'm going to do a perimeter sweep."

He lifted his right hand and gave a Cub Scout salute by touching his forehead with his index and middle fingers pressed together. He could feel Brenda's gaze on his back as he walked out the front door. She'd have more questions. It seemed in her nature to be inquisitive. As long as she didn't probe too deep, they'd get along fine.

"Something's up with my parents. Dad doesn't look good," Brenda confided to Kyle later that evening when they were alone. Her parents had retired, leaving her and her bodyguard alone in the living room.

Here she was hiding at her parents' house from some madman bent on hurting her, she had an annoyingly handsome protector by her side and her parents weren't being straight with her.

She'd taken one look at her father when she'd arrived this afternoon and known he'd had a fever.

It was infuriating to stand by while her dad was sick and not be allowed to treat him. They'd spent tons of money for her to become a doctor, and though her specialty was general surgery, she was still an experienced physician able to do more than just cut people open. It hurt that even in this she didn't measure up.

"You think it's more than a cold," Kyle said, his voice low. Light from the overhead track shone on him, shadowing his handsome features, making him appear mysterious.

Feeling a bit awkward with Kyle so close, she sat on the love seat, putting some distance between them. "They've both been acting so strange lately. We usually have Sunday dinner together, but the past two weeks they've canceled, saying they had something come up unexpectedly. A golf tournament one weekend and a retirement party the next. But…I'm not sure what to think. Dad's lost a lot of weight. He's never been heavy, but now he's almost gaunt, haggard even." Nothing like the stalwart, healthy man who'd taught her to sail.

"They're your parents. Parents tend not to want to worry their children with their problems. Tomorrow you can ask more questions and press for answers."

She heaved a sigh. "I suppose you're right. I just wish I could do something now."

"There's nothing you can do tonight. He's resting, and so should you." Kyle held out his hand.

She slid her hand into his, and the roughness of his palm rubbed against hers, creating friction. Sparks shot up her arm as he helped her to her feet. Not unpleasant but very surprising. How could just holding someone's hand create such chaos inside her? She'd never experienced anything like it before.

She extracted her hand. "You told my father you were ex–special operations for the Navy. What exactly does that mean?"

He wiggled his eyebrows. "It means I'm special, in a good way."

She shook her head. He'd been charming to her mother and respectful to her father all evening. But with her, he was the jokester. Why didn't he want to talk about himself? Most men she knew did. "Seriously. What did you do in the Navy?"

"Swim."

Exasperation sharpened her tone. "You're not going to tell me, are you?"

His expression turned earnest. A look she liked on him. "I really did swim. My specialty was underwater reconnaissance and demolition."

It sounded dangerous. But then she already knew he was a man who sought the rush, the buzz, of danger. It made for a great protector but not the type of guy a woman could pin her heart on. If she were interested in pinning her heart on any man. Which she wasn't. "I'll say good night now."

"I'll see you to your room," Kyle countered. "After you." He gestured toward the staircase.

He wasn't kidding when he'd said he was sticking close. "I hardly think anything's going to happen to me on my way to my room."

"I'm cautious. Plus, I need to know where you are. Just in case."

Just in case the lunatic after her tried something here in her parents' home. She rubbed her arms, fighting back a shiver of fear. "My room's the first one at the top of the stairs."

She led the way upstairs. At her bedroom door, Brenda asked jokingly, "Do you need to check the room?"

One corner of his mouth lifted. "What a good idea."

Her mouth gaped. She hadn't meant for him to actually do it.

He reached around her to open the door and brushed past her to enter the room. A second later he reappeared at the doorway. "No bad guys."

"That's reassuring." She met his gaze.

The light from the hall heightened the blue of his eyes. They reminded her of a summer sky reflecting off Lake Michigan. The sudden longing to be out on the water, gliding through the waves, the sound of sails filling with the wind, gripped her.

Just her and the boat on open water as far as the eye could see.

She heard herself sigh. Saw the slow spread of a smile lighting up his face and realized what he must be thinking. Heat crept up her neck and into her cheeks. She was not sighing over him. But telling him that would only sound lame. And make her sound like an idiot. "Good night, then."

He set his hands on her shoulders. She sucked in a quick breath. Twin points of heat seared her flesh from where he gripped her with strong hands. With gentle pressure, he moved her aside so he could step into the hall.

A fresh wave of embarrassment flushed through her. She'd been blocking his path out of her room. He must think her a complete airhead. Or worse, that she didn't want him to leave her alone.

Well, okay, maybe a part of her didn't want him to go too far away. For safety reasons. Just in case. And if she kept telling herself that, maybe it would be true.

"Good night, Brenda. Sleep well," Kyle said with a two-fingered salute.

She nodded like a bobblehead doll and watched him saunter down the stairs and disappear into the dark.

She sagged against the door frame. She had to get a

grip. She would *not* be interested in her bodyguard. No matter how attractive he was. He was a danger junkie. Only here to protect her. Period. She wasn't looking for a romance, a relationship or anything in between. With him or any man.

She'd been down that rocky path before and found herself at a dead end. She was not going there again.

As she slipped into her room and closed the door, she only wished her heart would stop racing every time he was near. It was only a biological response to an attractive man, but it sure felt like something more. Something she had no intention of pursuing.

After one more perimeter check, Kyle was satisfied the grounds of the Storm house were as secure as they could be with only the eight-foot-high laurel hedges as a barrier to the outside world. He dialed Trent offices. He stood in the shadowed driveway, listening to the ring of the cell phone pressed to his left ear, while keeping his gaze on the street. A few lights dotted houses down the block. Several houses over a parked car sat at the curb.

"Trent Associates, Simone speaking. How can we help?"

"Hey, it's me," Kyle said by way of greeting. The former Detroit homicide detective had joined Trent Associates around the same time he had. "How's it going?"

"All's quiet here," she replied. "Everyone's out in the field except me and James. How's your assignment?"

"Interesting." He quickly filled her in on Brenda and the case. "I need a couple of things checked out. Can you help?"

"Of course, anything for my favorite frogman."

"Ah, you're gonna make me blush," he quipped. From the day they'd met they'd had a good-natured banter going. Simone was all sleek polish. While he was...well, himself. They couldn't be more opposite. Brenda, in fact, reminded Kyle a little of Simone. The same quick wit and standoffish manner.

"First up a Dr. Sam Johnson, plastic surgeon at Heritage Hospital. Has a thing for Brenda and doesn't seem to understand no. He's probably not our perp, but maybe someone close to him wants Brenda out of the picture. Dig up whatever you can."

"Got it. Next?"

"Her parents. I need everything you can find on them."

"Wait, you want me to do a deep dig on her family? You think they're behind the attempt on your protectee's life?"

"No, I don't," he said. "But there's something off. I've got a gut feeling that there's more going on than they are saying. Mrs. Storm was quick to hide some medication when we arrived unexpectedly. Brenda says they've been acting strange lately. According to Brenda, her dad's lost a lot of weight and was feverish tonight."

"All right. I'll do some digging, though you know with HIPPA I won't get far on the medical," Simone said. "Anything else?"

Kyle hesitated. Something niggled at the back of his mind, but he couldn't put a bead on what was bothering him. "I'm good for now. But I'll call if I have anything else."

"Sounds good. Hey, Kyle?"

"Yeah?"

"Stay safe. I'm praying for you."

He smiled, glad to know someone was putting in a good word with the man upstairs. Kyle prayed often, but sometimes God felt so very distant. Kyle had come to know the Lord at the Special Warfare Center in Coronado, California. There were days when his faith was the only thing that sustained him through the vigorous training and later combat. "You're concerned about me? How sweet."

He heard her exasperated sigh. "As I am for every member of the team."

Kyle sobered. "I know. And I'm grateful."

"Be careful."

She'd shared her story with him after a harrowing assignment had left another team member in the hospital with a bullet wound. She'd lost someone close to her, someone she felt responsible for. Simone took everyone's welfare very seriously. He appreciated that about her. "I will. You, too."

"Thanks."

Kyle hung up and stared at the house shrouded in darkness, his hinky alarm jangling. Just what were the Storms hiding? And was their secret the reason Brenda was in danger?

The house was quiet when he came back inside. Only the faint hum of the refrigerator and the slight creaking of the floorboards settling for the night kept the place from being completely silent. Kyle swept the downstairs, making sure all windows and doors were locked tight and the security alarm was set. He headed to the guest room on the main floor near the kitchen.

The room was done in muted tones of green and brown. More masculine than not, yet it wouldn't necessarily be considered a man's domain, not with the bits of lace on the cherry dresser, the painting of a field of flowers and a lazy creek on the wall and the ruffles on the accent pillows he'd tossed onto the wingback chair in the corner. Still, as digs went, this was cushy and more than adequate to provide a good night's sleep.

He stretched out on the queen-size bed with every intention of relaxing. But his mind wouldn't shut off. He kept reliving the moment upstairs when Brenda had sighed. Such a small sound, hardly worth noting. Except she'd been staring at him with such yearning on her pretty face, his ego had ripped the curl. He'd wanted to explore what that sigh meant. He hadn't. And told himself he couldn't. That wouldn't be professional.

Giving up on sleep, he rose and dug through his "to-go" bag, double-checking his weapon and ammo. His hand brushed over the photograph he always kept with him. He didn't need to see the image to recall the picture of him, his twin sister, Kaitlin, and his parents. Before his mother had taken ill. Before his world came crashing down in a fiery flame of heartache. He zipped the bag closed.

A high-pitched noise pierced the quiet of the night.

His heart jolted.

The house alarm had been tripped!

THREE

Kyle palmed his SIG P226. As he opened the bedroom door, a rush of adrenaline sucked the breath from his lungs. Leading with his weapon, he stepped out into the hallway, prepared to face any intruder and do his job and protect Brenda. No matter what.

His eyes adjusted to the darkness. The alarm continued to blare, noise ricocheting off the wall and assaulting his ears. He moved quickly toward the staircase. Muted light from outside streamed through the wide-open front door. Dread flooded him.

One thought reverberated around his mind—he had to get to Brenda.

Please, God, don't let me fail her.

The silent plea tore from him as it did every time he was responsible for another's life.

Sudden light flooded the stairwell. Kyle blinked as Brenda ran down the stairs, nearly colliding with him as he hurried up. At the sight of her, a surge of relief loosened the knot in his gut. He snaked an arm around her waist to halt her forward motion. Her bare knees knocked against his below the loose basketball shorts he wore. "You okay?"

"Yes." Her small hands gripped his biceps. "Why's

the alarm going off?" she yelled above the shrill ringing of the house alarm.

"Don't know." Her body trembled against him, making him acutely aware of how adorable she looked in plaid shorts and a green tank top that hugged her curves.

Her hair hung over her shoulders, making her appear young and vulnerable. And in need of protection. Protection not just from the bad guys but also from him. He set her away, needing some distance so he could focus.

Moving so that Brenda was behind him, he approached the front door, careful to keep them out of the line of sight in case a sniper lay in wait, ready to pick them off.

Motioning to the alarm pad on the wall, he said, "Take care of that."

With quick fingers, she punched in the alarm code. Blessed silence filled the house. Kyle peered around the doorjamb to the front walkway. Two figures huddled together on the driveway.

"Stay put," he ordered Brenda before venturing out the door, his gun raised and sighted.

He reached the porch stairs as recognition flooded his brain. He lowered his weapon. Brenda pushed past him. He reached out with his free hand to halt her. "I said stay put."

She sidestepped his reach and ran down the drive. "Mom? Dad?"

Kyle growled in frustration and hurried after her. He halted beside the older couple. Sweat beaded Mr. Storm's brow and soaked through his cotton nightshirt. Mrs. Storm held on to his arm as if he might fall if she let go.

Kyle's gaze searched the grounds. He didn't see any

threat or danger. But that didn't mean one wasn't out there. "Let's take this inside."

"Sorry about the alarm. I forgot to unarm it," Mr. Storm said, his voice strained. "I needed some fresh air."

Brenda touched her father's forehead. "You're burning up again."

He captured her hand. "I'm fine. I just took some ibuprofen."

"Dad—"

"Enough, Brenda."

Mr. Storm's sharp tone raised Kyle's defenses and brought back memories of his own father. The harsh, cruel way he'd spoken to both Kyle and his sister. The way Kaitlin would cower, retreating behind a wall of silence until there was a time Kyle feared she'd never speak again.

It had been up to Kyle to protect his sister. He'd failed her. He wouldn't fail Brenda.

He took a half step forward before he realized he had moved. Reason slammed into him. He shoved his SIG into the waistband of the basketball shorts he slept in and fisted his hands. It wasn't his place to intervene between his protectee and her parents unless they posed a physical threat.

Hurt flashed in Brenda's eyes, but she didn't back down. Good for her, Kyle thought. She was as tough as she was prickly. "Mom, run a tepid bath. We need to cool him down."

Mr. Storm growled. "Brenda—"

Mrs. Storm nodded, looking relieved to have her daughter taking over, and hurried back inside.

Brenda nudged her way beneath her father's arm and wrapped her other arm around his waist.

"What are you doing?" her father demanded.

Ignoring his protest, she said, "Come on, let's get you upstairs. Kyle, a little help, please."

Kyle moved around to Mr. Storm's other side.

"I'm not an invalid. It's just a cold," Mr. Storm groused.

They helped Mr. Storm into the house and up the stairs to the master bedroom, where they eased him onto the edge of the bed. The sound of water filling the tub came through the open door to the adjacent bathroom.

"Kyle, stay with him. I'm going to see if we have some juice. He needs to stay hydrated," Brenda said and left the room.

"I don't want her to see me like this," Mr. Storm said, his voice shaking. He seemed to have deflated in the past couple of seconds.

"You're sick. And it's not a cold," Kyle stated, watching the man closely. Would he keep up with the pretense?

Mr. Storm shook his head. "Cancer."

The word struck Kyle in the gut. Empathy squeezed his lungs. Images of his mother's final days played in his head. She'd been so weak and in pain. Only ten years old, Kyle hadn't understood. Now he did. And he wouldn't wish what his mom had been through on his worst enemy.

"I'm sorry. You need to tell Brenda."

"No! I don't want to burden her with this."

The noise coming from the bath stopped.

Kyle stared. "She's going to find out eventually. It would be better for her to hear it from you."

"She has enough to deal with right now."

Mrs. Storm entered the room and sat beside her husband. Taking his hand, she said, "He's right, Andrew. You have to tell her. Everything."

"There will be time enough later."

"Tell me what?" Brenda asked as she entered the room, holding a glass of orange juice. She gave the glass to her father. His hands shook as he lifted the glass to his lips and drank.

Concern arced, making Brenda's chest ache. "What do you need to tell me?"

Brenda hadn't wanted to admit even to herself how much her parents had aged since she'd last seen them, nearly a month ago now. Her father's hair had thinned, the gray more noticeable now. Her mother's drawn expression, the tired lines around her mouth and eyes, spoke of sleepless nights and stress.

Her parents exchanged a look. Her father gave a negative shake of his head. Her mother nodded with intensity.

Anxiety tripped up Brenda's spine. Whatever they were keeping from her wasn't good. That she'd already come to understand. But just how bad?

She braced herself. "Please."

Her father's shoulders sagged. He lifted his gaze. The look of sorrow shadowing his eyes caught her breath. He father had always been so strong, so vibrant. To see him looking so vulnerable tore at her, tilting her world even more out of balance. As if it wasn't already totally skewed with some madman wanting her dead.

"Dad? Mom? What's wrong?"

Her father looked away.

"Sweetie, your father is very ill."

She'd known they weren't being straight with her about his cold. She swallowed. "Go on."

"Colon cancer. Stage three."

Brenda mentally recoiled. Everything inside of her wanted to deny her mother's words. Not her father. He couldn't be sick. Agony ripped her insides to shreds. She struggled to take a breath, finally managing to ask, "A, B or C?"

"A."

That was something at least. A better survival rate. "When was the diagnosis made?"

Guilt flashed across her mother's face. "Two weeks ago."

"Two weeks," Brenda repeated, feeling as if she'd taken a blow to the gut. "You've known for two weeks, and you didn't say anything?"

"We didn't want to worry you, dear." Tears streamed down her mother's face.

The daughter in her wanted to cry right along with her mother, but the doctor in her kicked in, shoring up her emotions so she could deal with this crisis.

"Who are you seeing?" Brenda directed the question to her father.

When he didn't answer, her mother did. "Dr. Krember."

"He's one of the best." Brenda was thankful for that. "Surgery?"

"Scheduled."

"How soon?"

"Next week."

"That's unacceptable. I'll talk to Dr. Krember. He'll get you in tomorrow."

Her father's gaze whipped to her. "You'll do no such thing."

"But Da—"

"No. You'll stay out of it. This is another reason why

we didn't tell you. You'll want to take over, be in control like you always do. You have enough to deal with. This is my problem. Let me deal with it my own way." He stood, wobbled a bit, but then gained his balance. "Good night."

Hurt pierced her. Tears burned the backs of her eyes. Her heart felt as if it was cracking down the middle. Her father didn't want her help. He wanted her to stay out of his problem. They didn't think she could handle her job and her worry.

Didn't he understand how much she loved him? How much she wanted to be able to take care of him? When would she be good enough?

Her parents disappeared into the bathroom. The door shut firmly with a snap.

Brenda closed her eyes. Tears leaked from the corners. She forced back the pain with practiced precision.

A hand touched her shoulder. Kyle.

She couldn't take his sympathy or his irreverent humor at the moment. She felt too vulnerable, too needy, and she hated that.

She needed to be alone. Needed to come to terms with this devastating news on her own. Needed to get out where she could gather her control.

She whirled and ran from the room, feeling as if her world had imploded and would never be the same again.

Kyle closed the master-bedroom door behind him. The Storms needed their privacy. His heart ached for them. He understood all too well the pain they were dealing with.

He also understood how Brenda was feeling. More so. He'd been shattered when his mother had finally confessed she was dying. The trips to the doctors' offices and the hospital hadn't cured her of the disease robbing her of life.

He could remember sitting in the waiting room while his mother had treatment after treatment, not understanding the severity of her condition or the probable outcome. Not realizing that their time together was running short.

Hoping to offer her some comfort, he walked down the hall to Brenda's closed bedroom door and gently knocked.

She didn't answer. "Brenda?"

Still no answer. She had a right to her privacy as she dealt with the horrible news she'd heard. Yet, he hesitated to leave without checking on her. Some elemental instinct compelled him to take action. He tried the knob. Unlocked. He pushed the door open, half expecting to find her weeping on her bed. But she wasn't on the queen-size bed or sitting on the wingback chair in the corner. She wasn't in the room at all.

Alarm spiraled through his system. Not knowing where his protectee was at all times left her open to attack. He bolted down the stairs. Not in the kitchen. Nor the living room. He checked the guest room just in case she'd sought refuge in his space.

The front door was closed. The green light on the alarm indicated it wasn't set. He ran for the front door. No sign of her in the driveway or the lawn. He sprinted around to the back of the house. Not there, either. Apprehension urged him back to the front of the house and out into the street.

The houses of the residential neighborhood were dark and quiet. The street was empty except for a car parked four houses down. Trees lining the sidewalks obscured the view. Kyle wished he had night-vision goggles with him.

On the other side of the street, between the trees, the silhouette of a person caught his attention. Brenda. She was walking at a fast clip along the sidewalk. Faint snatches of moonlight caught on her hair, making the dark strands glisten like jewels against velvet.

The ping in his veins turned to pounding. He ran to catch up with her. "Brenda, wait," he called in a stage whisper.

She halted, her arms wrapped around her middle.

When he caught up to her, he snagged her elbow. "Let's get something straight right now. I don't care what's going on, you cannot go off alone."

She didn't say anything but stood frozen in place. Sympathy infused him, making his heart ache for her. She'd been delivered a shocking blow. One he would imagine was doubly difficult, considering she was a doctor and knew what the diagnosis entailed. Still her life was in danger. They couldn't get careless. He placed an arm around her shoulders and steered her back toward the house.

"Why did they keep this from me?" she whispered, her voice thick with tears.

A flippant remark about parents being from another planet, playing by different rules, rose, but he squelched it. She needed his compassion, not his wit. Too bad he didn't have a reason to give. "I'm sure they thought they were doing the right thing."

"By keeping something this important from me?"

"I'm not saying they were right." He didn't know how to help her come to terms with the news. Dealing with a protectee's emotions wasn't normally part of his job description, beyond the occasional reassurance. Most of his protectees preferred to have their protection detail be a silent but visible deterrent. But in Brenda's case, that wasn't an option.

He needed to stick close to her, become a part of her everyday world, until they caught the person threatening her life. Opening up about his own life seemed to be a prudent choice. One he hoped would help her trust him. Trust him enough to listen to him when it came to her security. "When my mother was sick, my parents never said a word until the end."

Brenda stopped and turned to face him. "You lost your mother?"

The sympathy in her tone revived some of the old pain. He'd rather relive the worst of SEAL training than experience losing his mom again. "I was ten when she passed."

Brenda touched his arm. The point of contact created an epicenter of warmth that spread up his arm. "I'm so sorry. What did she have?"

Emotion clogged his throat. Even after all this time, he still got choked up. He tucked Brenda's hand around the crook of his arm and walked back toward her parents' house. He kept his eyes trained on the shadows, his senses alert for any threat. "When my mom was about five, my grandparents' house burned down. They all got out unburned, but the house was full of asbestos. They'd breathed it in. They all had problems after that. My grandparents died before I was born."

"Pleural mesothelioma," she explained, her measured words full of sympathy. "The asbestos caused scar tissue that limited the exchange of oxygen to the bloodstream."

"Yes." He still remembered the way his mother gasped for breath. Even with an oxygen tank, she couldn't seem to fill her lungs. "It's a painful way to go."

From down the street the sound of an engine turning over echoed in the quiet of the night. Reacting swiftly to the sound and its meaning, Kyle pulled Brenda into the shadows behind the thick trunk of a large maple tree.

"What's happening?" Brenda asked.

He pressed his index finger against her lips. "Shh. Be still."

His gaze scanned the road. He could barely make out the car rolling slowly down the street without its lights. As the older sedan moved past where they stood in the shadows, Kyle concentrated on the driver. A hoodie covered the person's head and obscured the facial features, but from his size he had to be a dude. The car continued on down the road. Red lights glowed as the car braked and made a right turn, disappearing from view.

There'd been no license plate on the car.

Not a good sign.

"Let's get you inside." He tugged her forward and hurried her across the street and up the drive.

Kyle caught Brenda by the elbow as she moved to the sink to sterilize her hands. "Are you sure you're up for this?"

The familiar sounds and smells of the hospital soothed Brenda's frayed nerves. She was about to step into her first surgery of the day, the removal of a gallbladder on a twenty-three-year-old woman who presented with cholecystitis, an acute inflammation of the gallbladder.

Brenda understood why he'd ask. She'd taken one look in the mirror this morning and nearly crawled back in bed. Her eyes were red and puffy, her skin pale with worry. But shirking her responsibilities wasn't an option. Her patients relied on her.

"I'm fine. Really," she answered. But she wasn't.

Her father was very ill.

His heartbreaking prognosis was a deep sorrow embedding itself in her soul.

The thought of what life would be like without her dad in the world left her feeling hollow and cold. She looked up to her father, strived to make him proud. As CFO of a major corporation before his retirement, he'd been the epitome of success to Brenda.

He'd grown up on a farm in Wisconsin, moved to Chicago to study at Northwestern University, graduated from the business school with honors and was hired on as an accountant's assistant with Penderson and Gutheries, a financial services corporation based in Chicago.

Her dad had worked his way up the food chain, just as Brenda planned to do in the hospital. Though she didn't share her father's head for numbers, she was a star pupil just like him. They both were valedictorians in high school, both graduated top of their class from the same college.

As a child she'd craved his attention and approval, always determined to do better, be better, but always feeling that somehow she wasn't living up to his image of an ideal daughter. It wasn't anything overt, just this vague sense of displeasure. When he showed her how to sail, she'd read everything she could on sailing for days before their lesson so she'd be able to keep up as he taught. But instead of being proud, he'd seemed disappointed she'd known so much already when they'd set out.

And even more disappointed when she decided she liked the one-person craft better than a team yacht.

She'd been too afraid he wouldn't understand if she explained how terrified she was she'd mess up on a team craft and disappoint him even further.

Last night had only intensified that feeling of inadequacy when he'd shunned her attempts to help. Logically she knew he was proud of her accomplishments. She'd heard him brag about her often to his golf buddies. Then why push her away?

She hoped they'd have time before it was too late to reconcile the disparity.

"Brenda?"

Kyle's deep voice shook her out of her dark reverie. She turned her gaze on him, feeling slightly disoriented. "Yes?"

"I asked if you need anything before you go in," he said, his gaze probing her face.

She started, realizing she'd spaced out for a second. The uncharacteristic moment shook her. She was in the scrub room, preparing to take an organ out of a patient. She'd better pull it together. The last thing she wanted was to be unfocused during a procedure.

She breathed in, filling her lungs, and slowly let the air out as she centered her mind and immediately realized she was thirsty. Not surprising, really. She hadn't drunk her normal sixteen ounces of water this morning because she'd been distracted by her bodyguard and her parents.

Her mother had made breakfast as if nothing catastrophic had shaken their world. Her father had sat at the kitchen table and read the paper. And Kyle had woofed down the eggs and bacon with gusto. Brenda had pushed her food around her plate but had no appetite. Sitting around acting as if her world wasn't falling apart literally made her sick to her stomach.

But her patient shouldn't suffer because of Brenda's personal problems. "A glass of water would be helpful."

Kyle nodded and padded to the water cooler in the scrub room. Gratefully she took the cup he offered when he returned and drank the liquid.

"Thank you," she said when she handed back the empty cup, feeling better already.

"More?"

She smiled, appreciating his solicitousness. "No, I'm good. Thank you."

After scrubbing her hands, she entered the O.R. Her patient lay prepped on the table, white cloths placed so that only a square patch of her abdomen was exposed. The anesthesiologist, Derek, sat at the head of the table monitoring the patient's vitals while the surgical technician prepped the instrument tray and laparoscopy, the video camera that would guide Brenda once she'd made the incision.

Brenda barely noticed the room itself. Bare, sterile walls. Cold metal everywhere. The faint odor of cleaner permeated the air.

One nurse, Kate, stood a few paces back. A second nurse approached Brenda with gloves and mask at the ready.

"How's our patient this morning?" Brenda asked as the nurse slipped the gloves quickly over Brenda's fingers and then secured the face mask behind her ears.

"Out like a light and waiting," the nurse answered. "She was a bit nervous when we spoke earlier, but I told her she had the best surgeon in the city working on her today."

"Thanks, Marge." It was high praise indeed coming from the veteran nurse. They'd worked alongside each other often the past few years, ever since Brenda came on board at Heritage as a resident. She liked having Marge as her scrub nurse. She was competent, assertive in technique, anticipating Brenda's needs before Brenda even had to ask. All good traits in a head nurse.

Though Brenda knew she was on the young side for a surgeon doing her fellowship under the auspicious guidance of one of the country's leading general surgeons, Marge had never made her feel inadequate. Here at the hospital, at least, people appreciated how hard she worked, the hours she dedicated to the patients.

Here going above and beyond was rewarded. One day when she became chief she'd make sure to continue the tradition of recognizing hard work.

Marge leaned close. "Who's the handsome stud by the door?"

Brenda glanced over to where Kyle had parked himself by the door. Handsome? Yes, Brenda couldn't deny the assessment even if she wanted to. He was dressed from head to toe in green surgical scrubs just as she was, but the drab outfit didn't detract from the width of his shoulders, the trim waist and long, lean legs. A face mask covered his mouth and nose. Gloves encased his strong hands, and shoe covers hid the loafers he wore.

Only his watchful blue eyes were visible. Beautiful eyes. Intense. Protective. Alert. Eyes that seemed to see a little too much for her comfort level. Brenda shifted her gaze back to Marge. "Bodyguard."

Above her mask, Marge's hazel eyes widened. "Bodyguard?"

Obviously the hospital gossip party line hadn't reached the nurse. Relief that she wasn't the butt of watercooler speculations and assumptions swept through her.

"Long story. I'll explain later." She stood beside the

prone young woman lying on the operating table. "Let's get to work."

An hour into the procedure, a hissing sound disturbed Brenda's concentration. "What is that noise?"

"It's not coming from my end," Derek said, though he stood to check his machines.

Marge lifted her head toward the vents in the ceiling. "It sounds like it's coming from up there."

"I can't breathe," Kate said, her hands going to her throat a second before she crumpled to the ground, hitting the instrument tray on her way down, sending forceps, retractors and scalpels flying.

The startling clatter of the surgical instruments hitting the floor jolted through Brenda as she stared in horror at the fallen nurse.

Suddenly she didn't feel so good, either. Her eyes burned. The membranes of her nose tingled painfully. She lifted her hands away from the patient and glanced up. The vent was directly over her. A fine mist sprayed out of the slats. The room spun.

A loud siren drowned out the hissing noise. Someone had pulled the emergency lever.

In a heartbeat, Kyle was at Brenda's side, his arms encircling her, pulling her away from the table. "We need to get you out of here."

"My patient," Brenda protested though her words slurred. The room darkened. The floor slid out from under her feet. Falling. Kyle's strong arms caught her and lifted her against his chest. The scent of his aftershave chased away the stench of antiseptic and blood. She hoped she wasn't dying.

The world went black.

FOUR

Kyle refused to succumb to the mist flowing freely through the hospital ventilation system and flooding the operating room. He held his breath, his lungs straining against the lack of oxygen intake. His chest burned with the chemical agent. He forced his eyes to stay open. His mind to stay alert. His limbs to function.

Blood pounded in his ears, drowning out the alarm reverberating off the operating-room walls. Fogginess hovered at the edges of his mind, but he gritted his teeth, refusing to give in to the clawing need for air, and pushed through the pain.

He lifted Brenda in his arms. No time to check her pulse. Not with the lack of fresh air. He had to get them both out of here.

Each step took extreme concentration. Lift one foot, put it down. Then repeat. The door seemed a mile a way.

He blinked away the dark spots blotting out the light.

The door banged open. Someone wearing white from head to toe rushed to him. Reflexively he tightened his hold on Brenda. Turning his shoulder toward the oncoming assault, he continued moving, doing a little bull-rushing of his own.

But his legs gave out. No! He had to get her to safety.

Brenda slipped from his arms. His muscles wouldn't work, wouldn't hang on to her. He'd failed to protect her. The darkness descended, overwhelming the light. He let out a groan of protest as the world faded.

A clear plastic mask covered Kyle's face. Cool air swiftly filled his lungs, chasing away the lethargy. His nose and throat stung. He shook his head to clear his mind. He fought for clarity. They'd been in the operating room. A hissing sound. The smell of bleach. The fine mist of gas flooding the room.

Brenda!

He'd lost her.

He yanked off the mask and pushed himself upright. Blood rushed to his head. His vision narrowed then slowly cleared. He was on a bed behind a curtained wall. Standing took effort. The world wobbled then righted itself.

Brenda. He had to find her.

He pushed back the curtain. The emergency room buzzed with energy.

A nurse hurried toward him. "Sir, you really shouldn't be up yet."

Ignoring the nurse's admonishment, Kyle grabbed the nearest police officer. No doubt the incident in the operating room had brought the police in force. "Dr. Storm? Have you seen her? Is she okay?" *Oh, please God, let me have gotten her out in time.*

"Sir, are you all right? You don't look so good," the officer said.

An older man dressed in a brown suit stepped to Kyle's side. "Mr. Martin, I'm Detective Lebowitz, the lead on this case." He frowned. "You should sit down before you fall down."

Kyle cut the air with a frustrated hand. "No, I have to find Dr. Storm."

"She's being looked after by Dr. Landsem."

"I need to see her." Kyle wouldn't be at ease until he saw for himself that his client was safe. "Where is she?"

"This way." Lebowitz led the way down a hall.

Kyle kept a hand on the wall, fighting the dizziness camped out at the edges of his mind. They stopped at a private room. Lebowitz pushed open the door.

Brenda lay stretched out on a gurney, an oxygen mask covering her face.

A man dressed in a lab coat hovered at the side of the bed. Not Dr. Landsem. The killer come to finish off what he started?

Stark panic slammed into Kyle, wrenching his senses to high alert.

"Get away from her!" Kyle roared.

He grabbed the guy in a sleeper hold with his arm across the man's throat, creating a triangle, pressing on the carotid artery. Kyle spun him away from Brenda. The man's hands clawed ineffectively at Kyle's arm as the oxygen supply to the man's brain diminished. Kyle knew the guy's brain was going fuzzy just as his was from the residual effects of the gas.

"Mr. Martin!" Lebowitz had his gun drawn. "Step away from the doctor."

"He could be the one trying to kill her," Kyle ground out.

"Kyle?"

He lifted his gaze. Brenda stared at him from above the mask. Relief swamped him. She was alive.

"Let him go," she said in barely more than a hoarse whisper. The scratchy sound of her voice twisted Kyle up inside. The effects of the gas. A little longer in that room and her throat would have completely closed as the gas tore into her trachea and lungs, choking her. Killing her.

"Please, Kyle. It's Sam," she choked out.

The plastic surgeon who had a thing for Brenda.

Kyle eased the pressure on the guy's neck; he could still be her would-be assassin. He quickly patted him down. No weapon.

"Let. Me. Go," Sam croaked.

Kyle released him.

Lebowitz holstered his gun with a glare at Kyle. "That was not necessary."

"Can't take any chances," Kyle shot back, not caring that he'd acted swiftly. He'd rather apologize than have his client dead.

Sam clutched his throat and glared at Kyle. He wore a lab coat over pressed slacks and a pale pink button-down shirt. The name tag on his right breast pocket read Dr. Sam Johnson.

"Who are you?" Sam demanded to know.

"Someone who wants to keep Brenda safe," Kyle said.

"I wouldn't hurt her," Sam declared, clearly affronted by the suggestion.

Relegating Sam to a low-level threat category, at least in a physical, one-on-one match even with his brain fuzzy, Kyle shifted his attention to Brenda. "Hey, Doc."

She focused on his face and reached up to pull the mask off herself.

Sam crowded in. "Hi, Brenda."

Kyle held his ground, an immovable barrier keeping the plastic surgeon from getting too close.

"Dr. Johnson, maybe you should step out," Lebowitz said. Sam frowned, stepped back but didn't leave.

Brenda's gaze bounced between the men then stayed on Kyle. "What happened?"

"You passed out." He wanted the details as well but right now his priority was to get her out of there before her assassin made another attempt on her life. "We need to leave. Now."

Brenda clutched Kyle's forearm. "Tell me what happened."

Kyle turned to the detective. "Lebowitz?"

The detective cleared his throat. "We found a hose in the ventilation shaft leading to a bottle of bleach mixed with ammonia. The combination created a deadly gas."

Brenda gasped. Her panicked gaze locked on Kyle's. He could see she'd made the same connection he had the second he'd realized gas was being funneled through the vent. Someone with access to the hospital did this. Someone she probably knew and worked with.

"He got you out in time." Sam moved to the foot of the bed. He gave Kyle a disdainful once-over. "Though I'm not sure what he was doing in the O.R. in the first place." His tone reeked of censure.

"Mr. Martin was hired by the hospital to provide protection for Dr. Storm," Lebowitz said, his tone making it clear he approved.

"My patient?" Brenda asked.

"She was wearing an oxygen mask so she didn't breathe in any of the chemicals," Lebowitz stated.

"Dr. Landsem had her moved to another O.R.," Sam supplied. "He's closing her up right now."

"The others?" Kyle asked, directing his question to Lebowitz.

Lebowitz met his gaze. "One nurse is critical."

"Derek thought quickly," Sam said. "He put on an oxygen mask before hitting the alarm. He dragged Marge out."

When he didn't continue, Lebowitz said, "By the time we got to the other nurse…" He shook his head. "She didn't make it."

"Oh, no." Brenda sank back to the bed. The weight of responsibility bowed her shoulders. Kate. Dead. Another death on her conscience. "What have I done?"

"Hey." Kyle placed a hand on her shoulder and gave a warm, gentle squeeze. "This isn't your fault."

She lifted her gaze. He towered over her. The glow from the overhead lights outlined his blond hair. He needed a haircut, she thought inanely. She blinked back the tears threatening to spill down her cheeks. She normally wasn't so weak as to give in to tears. But then she'd never been in a situation like this, where innocent people were being hurt, killed, because of her. "It should have been me."

A scowl darkened Kyle's handsome face. "No. No one should have died today." The hard note in his voice sent a shiver down Brenda's spine. "The nurse's death is on the person who rigged the poisonous gas."

Logically she knew that was true. But if she hadn't come to work, if she hadn't been in that operating room today, if she hadn't done whatever it was that attracted some crazy nut's attention…Gary the security guard and Nurse Kate would be alive.

She tried to stand, but her stomach lurched and her legs shook. Kyle helped her to her feet and tucked her into his side, his arm holding her close. She felt protected, as if he was a shelter in a storm. Yet she hated that she wanted, needed, that protection. The hospital, the one place she'd always felt at home in, now posed a threat to her life and those she worked with. The tragedy with the cupcakes had come from outside the hospital walls. This—the gas piped into her O.R.—had come from within. Like a cancer instead of a stalker.

She thought about the staff she'd worked with over the years. Was one of them out to get her? Why?

Or was the villain posing as a patient, biding his or her time, waiting for a moment to strike?

"Is there anyone you can think of who would want to hurt you?" the detective asked.

She shook her head and immediately regretted doing so as pain throbbed at her temples. "No. I don't know who or why someone would do these horrible things."

Tension emanated from Kyle like a high-voltage electrical current. He turned to Lebowitz. "I'm not liking how exposed she is here. Whoever did this has too much access to the hospital and the staff. You need to find the creep. Pronto."

Brenda shuddered and pressed closer to Kyle's side.

"We're doing our best." Lebowitz produced a notepad and pen from the inside breast pocket of his jacket. "Where can I contact you?"

Kyle took out a business card from his pants pocket and handed it to the detective. "This has my cell and the main number for Trent Associates. They always know how to reach me."

Lebowitz stuffed the card into the breast pocket of his suit jacket and then handed one of his cards to Kyle. "If you need anything—" he shifted his focus to Brenda "—or think of anything that would be helpful, please call."

Brenda tried to smile, but she feared it came out more like a grimace.

"Where are you taking her?" Sam asked, blocking their way.

"To safety."

Something in Kyle's expression made Sam draw back and move out of the way to allow them to pass. Brenda wanted to apologize to Sam. He wasn't the enemy. He was only trying to be a friend. But the words stuck in her throat.

People were dead because of her. She'd been so stubborn, so set in her ways and in her belief she could control this… It was better for Sam if he just let her go.

She realized she was shuffling down the hall in bloodstained scrubs and booties over her shoes. "I need some things from my office," she told Kyle.

His eyebrows dipped, but he nodded and led her to her office. She grabbed her purse, her pager and the files to the Hanson case. She made arrangements for someone to cover her shifts at the hospital and at the clinic.

"Now I'm going to the locker room to change out of these scrubs."

Kyle shook his head. "No. You can wait until we get to your parents'."

She stiffened, ready to argue, but then decided he was right. Better to just leave now rather than put herself or anyone else at risk. She turned off the light in the office. Her parents were going to be distraught by this latest attempt on her life. They had so much they were dealing with already; she hated to burden them with this, as well. And if anything happened to them because of her…

Grateful to be leaving the hospital on her own legs, Brenda slid her arm around Kyle's waist. Cocooned within his protective embrace, she wanted to believe she'd be safe. That he'd be able to keep her safe.

But she was afraid safety was nothing but a pretty illusion.

"We can't go to my parents'," Brenda said. She sat in the passenger seat of Kyle's SUV with her hands folded tightly in her lap. Her tense jaw and her dry-eyed gaze, full of determination, didn't bode well. "If anything happened to them because of me…" She looked away and swallowed. Then winced.

Empathy tightened Kyle's shoulder muscles. He slowed the vehicle and pulled to an angled stop at the curb. Keeping the SUV angled so the front end stuck out slightly forced other cars to swing wide, which put more distance between them and other vehicles as well as allowing a quicker, easier exit should anyone attempt to box them in. Staying alert to their surroundings, he kept the vehicle idling. An ambulance roared by, its siren blaring as it headed for the hospital a few blocks away. He understood Brenda's reluctance to return to her parents' home. Two attempts on her life had resulted in the death of two innocent bystanders, people she knew. She wanted to protect her mother and father.

"Then we'll have to go to your apartment for clothes and such, until I can arrange for a safe house."

"Good. Thank you." She dug into her purse and brought out her cell phone. "I'll call and let them know."

Kyle didn't envy that task. The Storms were dealing with a serious illness, and finding out that another attempt had been made on their daughter's life would only add to their stress. But there was no help for that if Brenda wanted to keep them safe. He made a U-turn and headed toward Brenda's neighborhood.

He listened to Brenda downplay the incident at the hospital to her parents, explaining the need to stay close to town in case there were further developments. He couldn't fault her for trying to minimize the seriousness of the situation so her parents wouldn't worry. When she hung up, he said, "You do realize you're evading the truth to protect them just as they kept your father's illness from you to protect you."

She frowned. "This is different."

"If you say so."

After a quiet pause, she said, "He can't control the illness."

"And you can control this?"

She made a face. "No."

"That's why I'm here," he reminded her.

"Exactly. You're trained at what you do. So am I. I'm a doctor. I should have been told about his illness. I could help him, make sure he's getting the best care possible."

"But he is getting the best care possible, right? You said his doctor was the best oncologist in town."

"True, but..." She closed her eyes for a moment. When she opened them, there was a bleakness to her gaze that ripped at him. "I feel so helpless." Anger colored her words. "There's nothing I can do for him, nothing he'll let me do for him."

Flipping on a blinker, Kyle changed lanes. "You could pray."

She cut him a sharp glance. "You think God will heal him?"

Doubt underscored her statement.

He met her gaze. "You don't believe that could happen?"

She sighed. "I—I don't know what I believe. I've

heard stories of people trusting God and getting better. I know my parents believe it's possible." She shrugged. "I've just never seen it happen."

He drove around the block twice, keeping his gaze alert for any threats. He didn't see any. "And you need to see it to believe it?"

She gestured with her hands as if to say, "What can I say?"

"I'm enmeshed in science. Theory must be proven to become fact."

He made a scoffing sound in his throat. "So you take nothing on faith?"

"Do you?" she countered, her laser-sharp gaze pinning him to the seat.

He thought about that as he parallel parked his rig at the curb outside her apartment building. He cut the engine and shifted toward her. He didn't normally share his faith with clients. That wasn't what he was hired to do. But since she asked… "I do. It took me a while to get there because I didn't grow up believing in God. But when I joined the Navy, I realized something was missing in my life. That something was faith. I know God's real, even if I can't see Him."

"That makes you and me very different."

"All it takes is being open and willing."

"I'm not there." She reached for the door handle. "I won't ever be there."

Her statement made him sad for her, but he wouldn't judge her. God would bring her to Him in His time. "Sit tight. I'll come around."

She sat back with a nod.

Exiting the vehicle, Kyle scanned the area for any potential hazards. Looking for anyone seeming too interested or trying hard not to appear interested, he searched for any manned cars idling nearby. None. He searched the rooftops, the windows of the buildings, the nooks and crannies that might provide cover for a shooter. Not finding anything worth noting as a threat, he opened the passenger door.

Brenda climbed out.

He immediately positioned her in front of him at arm's length, allowing him to see any upcoming threats to which he'd need to adjust and react to, and to protect her from possible attack from behind.

They reached the door of her apartment building. His hand on her shoulder, he kept her from entering. He went through first, assuring himself no danger waited within the lobby, then tugged her forward by the hand. They rode the elevator to the fifteenth floor. When the doors to the elevator slid open, he motioned for her to stay put as he stepped off, assessing the hallway. He hated the tight space. So many doors hiding possible threats. The corridor was empty. He motioned her out of the elevator. Keeping her positioned in front of him to his right, they went to her apartment door.

Brenda gasped.

The dead bolt had been punched through.

Someone had broken into her apartment.

FIVE

The buzz of adrenaline filled Kyle's head. Had the intruder come and gone? Or was there someone lying in wait inside the apartment like a spider stalking its prey?

Down the hall the elevator dinged. Someone was coming.

He pushed Brenda behind him and drew his weapon.

The elevator doors slid open but no one exited. The doors slid shut.

He didn't like how exposed they were in the hallway.

Heart pumping, Kyle pushed open Brenda's apartment door with his foot. No movement from inside. Leading with his weapon, he crossed the threshold and entered the apartment. Brenda's hand fisted the back of his shirt as she stepped in behind him.

"Oh, no," she said.

Her apartment had been trashed. His gut clenched with a mixture of anger at the violation but also relief that she hadn't been here to face the intruder.

Her couch had been ripped to shreds, the stuffing strewn all over the place. The photos on the walls were yanked off their hooks and smashed on the carpet. Glass from the frames glittered in the light streaming in through the open curtains.

Putting a finger to his lips, he motioned for her to remain quiet. The intruder could still be in the apartment.

He urged her into the kitchen, behind the dividing wall. The contents of the cupboards and drawers had been dumped out on the tile floor. Eyes wide, she crouched down, pushing at the discarded utensils to make room.

"Stay down," he cautioned quietly.

He moved through the apartment quickly. He found the same sort of destruction in her bathroom and bedroom. But no intruder.

"All clear," he said when he returned to the living room.

Brenda stood, her face ashen. "Why would someone do this?"

He went to her side. "This sort of destruction seems very personal."

He dialed 911 on his cell phone and explained the situation to the operator, asking for Detective Lebowitz to be contacted.

Taking her by the hand, he led her out of the apartment. Keeping his weapon ready, they approached the elevator. He pushed the down button then positioned them off to the side.

"We aren't going to wait for the police?" she asked, her voice tight.

"We'll wait downstairs. They'll need to process the scene."

The door of the elevator slid open. Kyle peered inside, ready to take out a bad guy if necessary. No one was inside, yet the fine hairs at the back of his neck prickled.

"But I need clothes," she insisted.

"Later." He let the doors slide closed and tugged

her past the elevator toward the stairs. "Keep close," he said and guided her down to the lobby without incident. They moved to a windowless section of the lobby to wait.

Within minutes Chicago police arrived. Kyle explained the situation. Three officers went up to secure Brenda's apartment and wait for the crime-scene unit to arrive to process the scene. Detective Lebowitz climbed out of a brown, nondescript sedan and hurried inside the building.

"Was there anything missing?" the detective asked after Kyle told him about Brenda's apartment.

Brenda shrugged. "I don't know. We didn't hang around long enough for me to account for everything."

"I'm taking Brenda out of here," Kyle said, grateful for the police presence that would deter any action on the part of Brenda's unidentified assailant. "She'll have to inventory the apartment later."

Detective Lebowitz patted his breast pocket. "I've got your contact info. I'll be in touch."

Keeping alert to any threats, Kyle escorted Brenda to his SUV.

"Where are we going?" she asked as he drove them out of the city.

Good question. He dug out his cell, punched the speed-dial number for Trent Associates and put the call on Speaker. Within a couple of seconds he had his boss on the line.

"Hey, boss, it's Kyle. I have a situation." He explained what had happened both at the hospital and at Brenda's apartment.

"Is the client all right?"

Kyle glanced at Brenda sitting so composed in the

passenger seat. She was holding it together. Impressively so. He arched an eyebrow when her gaze met his.

"Yes, I'm okay, sir," Brenda said.

Her calm voice surprised him. She'd come close to dying today, yet she was as cool as ice. Better than hysterics, he thought. He hated when his clients went all theatrical on him. He liked Brenda's composure. Probably came with the territory of being a surgeon. Steady under pressure.

"Good to hear that, Dr. Storm. I have every confidence Kyle will keep you safe."

James's praise meant a great deal to Kyle. There were very few men in the world Kyle looked up to. James was at the top of the list right next to Kyle's former commanding officer and Judge Fisk, the man who'd been instrumental in Kyle's decision to enlist in the Navy.

"It will take a couple of hours to arrange a safe house," James said.

"I have an idea, sir. Felicia Brewster has a lake house an hour and a half outside the city. We can go there."

Kyle could feel Brenda's surprised gaze.

"Very well. Check in when you arrive. And as always, if you need anything, you call," James said and hung up.

"Who is Felicia Brewster?" Brenda asked with a touch of wariness in her tone.

"A family friend." Kyle wasn't sure how to explain the complicated nature of his and his sister's relationship with Felicia Brewster. "I think you'll like her."

"Won't we be putting her in danger?"

He shook his head. "There's no reason for anyone to connect you to her. And I'll make sure we're not followed. If you aren't comfortable there, then I'll have James arrange something else."

After a moment, she asked, "You like your boss?"

Like was a mild term compared with the feelings Kyle had toward James. Surrogate father, respected mentor, a man Kyle would lay his life down for. "He's the best."

Curious about this man she was placing her life with, Brenda asked, "How did you end up working for Trent Associates?"

"My charm and good looks got me the job."

She caught sight of the wicked grin on his face. Her stomach muscles clenched. She rolled her eyes to downplay her visceral reaction. The man could be charming when he wanted to be and he was certainly good-looking, but he was also full of himself. She was sure he had women falling at his feet all the time. A real heartbreaker.

The kind of guy who could make a girl forget what was important, forget what she wanted out of life.

Forget that she didn't want to get emotionally involved. Especially not with a man who "liked to play the field," "keep his options open."

"I'm sure your boss saw something more than that," she said.

He laughed. "You'll have to ask him."

Curiosity urged her to press. "Was Mr. Trent a Navy man, too?"

"No. Marine. When he retired he opened his own protection agency."

"Are all of his employees ex-military?"

"Some are ex–law enforcement."

More interested in Kyle than she should be, she asked, "Why did you join the Navy?"

She had a hard time picturing this man taking orders without mouthing off. She doubted that would be tolerated in any branch of the military.

"It was either serve my country or serve time."

She blew out a frustrated breath. "Yeah, right."

The man never gave a straight answer. She seriously doubted he'd been forced to enlist. One, she knew that was an old practice long ago abandoned by the military. Second, Kyle didn't strike her as the criminal type. Irreverent and cocky, sure, but not deviant. He couldn't be those things as a bodyguard. Could he? A prickling of unease made her realize she didn't know this man well enough to be sure of anything. Yet she was trusting him. She had to give him the benefit of the doubt.

"You don't believe me?" he asked with amusement lacing his tone.

"Not really. But if you don't want to tell me, that's fine. It's not like we're friends or anything."

"Come on, now. I thought we were fast on our way to becoming friends."

"Hardly." But the idea of him as a friend… She didn't have to lose her heart to a friend.

"What? You already have enough friends?"

She shrugged. "Not many."

It was his turn to scoff as he changed lanes. "I can't believe that."

She cocked her head to the side. "Why?"

"Everyone has friends."

The confidence in his tone made her think he really believed what he was saying. She turned away to stare out the passenger window as a hollow feeling settled in the pit of her stomach.

Not her. She had colleagues, she had subordinates and she had acquaintances. But not friends. There were no confidants for her to share her dreams and wishes. Her secrets.

She'd never really had friends growing up, though not for lack of trying on her mother's part. Mom had arranged playdates and enrolled her in dance classes, art classes and Girl Scouts. She was always the odd one in the group. Tolerated, but not sought out.

While other little girls were into Barbies and makeup, she'd been dissecting frogs and growing bacteria in petri dishes for as long as she could remember. Instead of posters of the latest teen sensations hanging on her walls, she'd had the periodic elements table and pictures of Madame Curie. A total geek. A quirk that had never changed.

Even as an adult, she was viewed as an oddity.

Except when she did her work. At the hospital she was someone worthy of respect. Too bad it wasn't enough to fill the void she tried so hard to ignore.

Kyle's hand covered her hand. Startled, she reflexively tried to pull away. He held on, the pressure gentle and warm. Somehow soothing.

"I was two weeks shy of my eighteenth birthday when me and a couple guys were caught joyriding in a car that didn't belong to us," Kyle said.

She stared at his profile, feeling special because he chose to confide in her. "Uh-oh."

He flashed her a grin. "Yeah, uh-oh. Thankfully, it was my first offense. The public defender pleaded my case before Judge Fisk." He shook his head. "I'll never forget how that crusty old man stared me down from the bench. I thought for sure I was going to juvie. Or worse."

Brenda tensed. "But he gave you a choice? I thought

the military wouldn't allow enlistment as an alternative to criminal punishment?"

"They don't. Judge Fisk gave me community service as punishment and strongly suggested I enlist in the military as soon as I turned eighteen. Which I did."

"That was nice of him to be lenient."

"Yeah. An unexpected blessing."

She wasn't sure what to make of his steadfast faith. How could he believe so strongly in something he couldn't prove even existed? "And you chose the Navy."

"Seemed the logical choice given how much I love the water."

He slowed the SUV and took an off-ramp. A mall appeared up ahead. "Time to shop."

They went inside a popular department store. Soft music played through unseen speakers. The tile floors gleamed. The air smelled vaguely of perfume. Sales clerks smiled as they entered the women's clothing section.

Brenda halted just as she crossed the carpeted area marking the beginning of the department. "Do you need clothes?" she asked, hoping he'd say yes and they could each do their own shopping.

"Nah. I'm good. My bags are in the back of the SUV." He grinned. "Besides, helping you pick out clothes will be more fun."

Fun? Somehow that wasn't a word she'd have thought to use. Shopping for clothes was a torture that had to be endured. She'd discovered a few years ago the ease of online purchasing. She'd order a few outfits, try them on in the privacy of her own home and return what didn't work. Buying clothes was a necessity, not a pastime. But over the next hour she had to admit shopping with Kyle was more enjoyable than she'd have guessed. He had an eye for style and found numerous pieces that coordinated together, which she wouldn't have picked herself. She wanted only a few key pieces, not a whole new wardrobe.

"Really, Kyle, I just need two pairs of slacks, a couple of shirts and a pair of shoes," she said, dismayed to see the pile of clothes on the checkout counter when she came out of the dressing room wearing black slacks and a black jersey top.

He arched an eyebrow. "You need color. Lots of color. Reds look stunning on you," he said, retrieving a garnet silk blouse from the pile. "So does green and blue." He picked out two more tops. "And you need some jeans." He laid out the three pairs she'd tried on. "Which one?"

She couldn't decide. Each was distinctly different. One pair had rhinestone stitched on the pocket and had made her feel glamorous. Another pair had a dark wash with stitching that flattered her figure nicely. Then there was a sensible plain pair. Her hand hovered over the sensible pair.

Kyle handed the store clerk a credit card. "We'll take it all."

"No," she protested. "I don't need all of these."

"We might not be coming back to the city for a while. You'll need clothes."

The reminder of the danger she was in dampened her mood. "I'll pay you back."

He grinned. "I'll add it to my bill."

She wanted to argue but decided doing so would only encourage more flippant remarks. She'd make sure the hospital included the amount of the purchases in Kyle's fees. Snagging the receipts, she tucked them into her purse.

With three full shopping bags in hand, they left the store. The instant they stepped outside the confines of the department store, Kyle's jovial mood dissipated. He glanced around as if he was looking for someone to beat up.

"Everything okay?" she asked, totally spooked.

"I don't know." He drew her back inside the store behind a nearby pillar. "I'm going to bring the SUV close. Don't move from this spot."

Clutching the bags tight, she nodded. "I'm not going anywhere."

"This store's security is high quality. If someone approaches you, scream."

A shiver of dread skipped over her skin. She nodded and watched him stride purposefully from the store. She wondered what had him so agitated.

Kyle drove the Suburban right up to the door so that the passenger side was facing Brenda. He climbed out, came around the front and opened both the front and rear passenger doors before returning to where he'd left Brenda.

"Stay low and keep your head down," he said, drawing her out of the building and curling his body over hers.

The loud retort of gunfire blasted adrenaline through Kyle's system. The ping of bullets hitting the SUV rang in his ears. Brenda let out a yelp of distress.

The shots were close. Too close. He searched for the sniper. On the store rooftop he spotted the silhouette of a man and the unmistakable outline of a long-barreled rifle.

He'd known danger was near. Had felt that stirring of alarm that had never let him down. His commanding officer used to say it was God's way of keeping His soldiers out of harm's way. Kyle believed it with a deep certainty.

But how had they been found? He was sure they hadn't been followed. The only thing he could figure was Brenda's cell phone. She most likely had a GPS app loaded on it.

"Get in," Kyle shouted and pushed her through the open rear passenger door before slamming it shut. "Stay down!"

A bullet rammed into the side door panel. Kyle dived through the open front passenger door, his hand snagging the handle and jerking it closed behind him. He slid into the driver's seat, threw the car into gear and stomped on the gas. The rig shot forward. He swerved to avoid colliding with an oncoming car.

As cautiously as possible, he sped out of the parking lot, hung a quick right and quick left, hoping the evasive moves would thwart any attempts at tailing them. He sped through several intersections, bombed across the on-ramp to the freeway and drove north.

"Can I get up now?" Brenda asked from the floor between the seats.

"Yes. You're good."

Brenda sat up. The shock on her face squeezed Kyle's heart in a tight vise.

"How did he find us?" she asked.

"I assume you have a cell phone on you."

"Yes. I always carry it."

He'd underestimated their adversary. "Take the battery out of your phone."

"Okay. Why?"

"Have you downloaded any applications that help you find your phone if it's lost?"

"Yes." Realization dawned on her face. "You think that's how whoever is after me found us?"

"I do." Which meant whoever was after her had access to her cell network. They weren't dealing with an amateur here. That rifle he'd seen was military grade.

She held up the battery. "Now what?"

"You should also take out the SIM card and tuck it away. We'll dump the rest as soon as we find a place. I don't want to alarm you, but whoever tracked us also has access to everything on your phone."

"There's not much on there. A few phone numbers, mostly take-out restaurants, and my work calendar."

He let go of the steering wheel with one hand and took out his cell phone and popped out the battery. Just in case. He'd have to wait to inform Detective Lebowitz. "Most people live by the info on their cells."

His had all his contacts in the device. He'd be sunk if he'd lost the SIM card.

She shrugged. "I use it to make calls and keep track of my time."

"No texting, no email?"

"I use my office computer for email, and I don't text. My parents still have older-generation cell phones."

Her earlier comment about not having friends suddenly didn't sound as ludicrous as it had when she'd first said it. He was good at keeping people at arm's length, but even he had buddies he shot hoops with occasionally, pals to windsurf with. And of course a sister, as well as the other protection specialists at Trent Associates. They were a team. If any of them needed something, they'd all respond. It made him sad to think the doctor didn't have anyone in her life like that. It had to be awfully lonely.

Twenty minutes later, the highway sign indicated

Winthrop Harbor was the next exit. He moved over to the right-hand lane, watching the traffic behind him to see if anyone else moved over. No one did.

He took the exit. A large wooden sign with bright blue letters welcoming travelers to Winthrop Harbor marked the beginning of the village nestled along the shore of Lake Michigan. He pulled into the first gas station he came to. While the gas was pumping, he dumped Brenda's phone and battery in the waste bin. She got out and used the restroom inside the small quick mart. When she returned, she carried bottles of water and a bag of chips.

"Please tell me you paid cash," he said with a sinking feeling in the pit of his stomach.

"Yes. I watch enough TV to know credit and debit cards can be traced." She handed him a bottle of water. "Thought you might be thirsty."

Pleased by her thoughtfulness, he accepted the water and downed half the bottle in one long drink. He finished with the gas, paid and got back behind the wheel. Brenda offered him hand sanitizer before holding out the bag of sour cream and onion potato chips.

After rubbing his hands together, he took a handful of chips. "Thanks."

"One of my unhealthy pleasures," she stated and popped a chip into her mouth.

"Only unhealthy if not eaten in moderation."

"True. Which is why I rarely buy them. I could eat the whole bag in one sitting."

He laughed. "I'll have to remember you have a weakness for chips."

"Only this flavor. I can do without any others. Well, I do like ranch flavored, too. Oh, and salt and vinegar."

"Duly noted."

After the couple of days she'd had, it was good to see she wasn't wallowing in self-pity or so frightened she couldn't function. He hoped the police discovered who was after Brenda soon so she could get back to her life.

They passed through the main part of town, past residential houses on tree-lined streets with sidewalks and unfenced lawns. A very idyllic place. The kind that Kyle had never lived in. They passed the North Point Marina, the largest one on the lake with well over a thousand slips, and from the look of it most were occupied. There were large fishing boats, yachts of various sizes, sailboats and schooners. The water was dotted with boats of people out enjoying the beautiful fall day.

The road wound along the shore. A sign on the shoulder read they were passing the state border into Wisconsin. Ten miles later he turned down a gravel drive that led to a nice-size house tucked away among the trees. He'd visited Felicia's cabin only once before, many years ago. The place looked as he remembered. He parked and got out, breathing deep, taking in the fresh, pine-scented air. Felicia may not be here, but he knew where she kept a hidden spare key.

Brenda climbed out of the rig and gathered her purchases. "This place is lovely."

"It is. Peaceful, too." Kyle grabbed his duffel bag from the back and then followed Brenda up the wood-plank stairs. He knocked.

Felicia answered the door. She had long silver hair spilling over her shoulders, glasses perched on her nose and a round face. She wore a white puff-sleeved shirt and multicolored skirt that stopped at her ankles to reveal bare feet. A beaming smile broke out on her face. "Kyle. What a pleasant surprise."

Tenderness and affection for this older woman

squeezed Kyle's chest. "Hi, Felicia." He leaned in to kiss her cheek. "I'm sorry to barge in on you like this, but we need a place to stay for a few days."

Felicia's gaze bounced between him and Brenda. Curiosity and pleasure lit up her gray eyes. "Of course you can stay here. Please come in."

She moved aside so they could enter. The smell of meat simmering made his stomach grumble. He set their belongings on the bottom stair of the upper floor.

"This is my client, Brenda Storm," Kyle said. "Brenda, Felicia Brewster."

Felicia's eyes widened as she took Brenda's hand. "Client? Oh, dear. That must mean you're in trouble of some sort."

"Yes, I am," Brenda said. "I hope we aren't imposing too much."

"Not at all. I will do whatever I can to assist you," Felicia replied.

Kyle knew Felicia would do anything she could to help. She was that kind of woman. He quickly explained the situation to Felicia, who listened with rapt attention. When he was finished, she turned to Brenda. "You did the right thing in hiring Kyle."

Brenda shot him a glance. "I've come to realize that."

Her pretty eyes held a cache of emotions in the swirling depths. Trust and attraction held him enthralled as something intense flared between them. The moment stretched. The sound of Felicia's chuckles jerked him back to reality.

"Something smells delicious," he commented, needing something to say to redirect them all.

"Beef stew. I had a craving." Felicia smiled and shrugged. "I think God knew I would be having company. There's plenty. Come eat."

"May I use your restroom?" Brenda asked.

"Of course you may," Felicia said with a smile. "First door on the left down that hall."

Brenda hurried away.

When Brenda had shut the door behind her, Felicia turned to Kyle. "The doctor is a beautiful woman. And single, I take it?"

He laughed. "Yes on both accounts."

She grinned. "Good."

"There's nothing there, Felicia," Kyle assured her. "She's a client. Nothing more."

"If you say so," she countered and walked into the kitchen.

He did say so. Yes, Brenda was beautiful. Attractive. She was also determined, focused and competent. Compassionate and empathetic. All good traits for a doctor. For a woman.

He tried to remember why he'd ever thought the doctor prickly, but couldn't. Brenda was so much more than what she appeared, and if he wasn't careful, he'd find himself knee-deep in emotions he wasn't prepared to deal with.

A romantic relationship wasn't part of his assignment.

He had a job to do.

A client to protect.

Anything else would only be a distraction. He had to shore up his defenses for the long haul.

SIX

Brenda leaned against the bathroom door, the knob digging into her hip. She forced herself to breathe. The way Kyle had looked at her, the way she'd felt all shimmery inside, had her off balance. It was only attraction, she scolded herself. A biological response to a handsome man. Not anything to get all freaked out about.

Of course, add in out-of-kilter emotions. Look at all she'd been through lately. She'd been targeted for murder. Two people were already dead. She'd learned of her father's illness. All of which turned her senses upside down and made her judgment wacky.

No doubt what she was feeling was gratitude to Kyle for rescuing her and getting her to safety. Nothing more.

There couldn't be anything more.

He was only temporarily in her life.

She had her career to think about. Her life to think about. A romantic relationship wasn't part of the equation. At least not yet. Someday, she'd be ready to try again. But Kyle would be long gone by then.

After splashing some cold water on her face, she squared her shoulders and joined Kyle and Felicia in the kitchen.

"Brenda? Are you okay? You look a bit pale," Felicia said as she set a bowl of savory stew on the table in front of her.

"It's been a rough couple of days," she answered and took a sip of the tart lemonade Kyle had poured for her.

Felicia studied her. "You don't know who's behind these attempts on your life?"

Shaking her head, Brenda said, "No. I can only guess that it has something to do with the lawsuit." At Felicia's raised eyebrows, Brenda explained, "I am being sued. Or rather me and the hospital. I had a patient die during a routine procedure. The autopsy couldn't provide answers. The machines didn't register a problem until he stopped breathing."

"It was his time to go," Felicia said with certainty lacing her words.

Brenda's gaze shot from Felicia to Kyle and back to Felicia. "But he didn't have a heart problem. Had no signs of distress. Nothing."

"We can't always explain the things that happen in life," Felicia said, her voice gentle. "You have to trust God. He has a plan for each of us. Even this man and his untimely death."

Brenda drew circles in the thick stew with her spoon. She wasn't sure she believed in God, let alone trusted Him. Even though she'd attended Sunday school and church with her parents, she'd had a hard time understanding. The only Bible story she related to was Doubting Thomas. But he got to touch the scars. Frustration pounded at Brenda's temples. "It doesn't make sense."

"Life doesn't always make sense," Kyle interjected.

A truism she had a hard time accepting because it grated on her need for logical cause and effect. She'd gravitated toward surgery because it made sense to her.

Unexplained death and disease didn't make sense. God didn't make sense.

But who was she to argue that when these two clearly relied on God?

She envied them their faith. What would it take for her to believe?

She was almost too afraid to find out.

The next morning came too soon for Brenda. Sunlight streamed through the open curtain of the bedroom. She covered her eyes with one hand, hoping for a few more moments of sleep, a few more seconds of not having to face the reality that someone wanted her dead.

She hadn't realized how exhausted she'd been until she'd crawled into the comfortable bed last night and fallen into a dreamless sleep. A welcome surprise. She'd have figured a few nightmares for sure, given the events of the past few days.

A knock sounded at the door.

"Yes?"

"You up?" Kyle called.

"Just a minute." She scrambled out of the bed and threw on the clothes she'd taken off last night before padding barefoot across the room to open the door.

Kyle stood on the threshold, looking handsome in a long-sleeve blue chambray shirt, which made his eyes look bluer than the lake outside. One corner of his mouth tipped upward. "Morning, sleepyhead."

"What time is it?"

"Almost ten."

She blinked. She couldn't remember the last time she'd slept past eight.

"When you're ready, come on down for breakfast," he said. "Oh, and wear jeans and a long-sleeve shirt."

"Why?"

With a slow grin, he said, "Now, if I told you, it wouldn't be a surprise."

She made a face. "I've had enough surprises lately."

"You'll like this one," he said.

With that he disappeared, shutting the door behind him. For a moment she stood there undecided. She didn't normally follow orders blindly. She liked to know the reason behind decisions, behind procedures. Liked step-by-step instructions. But it seemed her life was in chaos and would be for the foreseeable future. Maybe learning to go with the flow would be a good thing.

She showered in the adjacent bathroom and put on the plain jeans, tucking her pager inside her waistband. Then she selected a deep emerald-green long-sleeve shirt that had three little buttons at the neckline. Not wanting to take the time to blow-dry her hair, she twisted the damp strands into a chignon and fastened the mass with a hair clip before heading downstairs.

Kyle smiled as she entered the kitchen. "Hope you like oatmeal."

"I do. I haven't had oatmeal since I was a kid."

"As heart-healthy as oatmeal is, that's hard to believe."

She shrugged. "Just not something I make for myself."

"I'm glad I could," he said and set a steaming bowl in front of her.

She poured a liberal amount of warm syrup over the top of the hot cereal and savored every bite. "This brings back memories. My dad loved oatmeal." Sadness invaded her good mood. "I'd like to call my parents."

He nodded and handed her his cell phone. She dialed their house. No one answered. She frowned and hung up. "Not home."

"You can try again later," Kyle said, taking the phone back.

"Thanks." Worry made her breakfast churn in her stomach. Where would they have gone on a Saturday morning with her father so ill? Maybe they were just out taking a walk. Getting some fresh air. Hoping that was the case, she took her empty dish to the sink. "Where's Felicia?"

"She went to the post office."

"Could we go into town? I need a few things," Brenda said.

He arched an eyebrow. "You need more clothes?"

She cut him a sharp glance. "No. I need a toothbrush, toothpaste, shampoo, razor, face cream—"

He held up a hand as if warding off a disaster about to happen. "Okay, okay. I get it. We'll go to the store while we're out."

After cleaning up their dishes, they left the house. Once Brenda was settled in the SUV, she said, "So are you going to tell me now where we're going?"

"Not yet."

Holding on to her impatience, she took in the scenery as he headed them into town. She'd never been to this little part of the state. It was quaint and very different from her world in Chicago. When he pulled the SUV into a parking spot in front of a store, she stared.

The outline of a hunter aiming a rifle at a big-antlered moose was painted on the outside of the store. "The Rifleman?"

"For all your hunting needs," he said and climbed out.

As he came around to the passenger door, she tried

to make sense of why he'd bring her here. Did he plan on taking her out in the wilderness?

He led her into the store, past all the various outdoor gear and supplies to the back of the building. The muffled retort of gunfire coming from the other side of a windowed wall sent a shiver of apprehension down her spine and made her quake in her new tennis shoes. There were five spaces set up with targets at one end. Three spaces were occupied. "A shooting range?"

Kyle stopped before a case of small handguns. "How're you doing?" he said to the guy behind the counter.

"Good. Yourself?" the big, burly man replied.

"Great." He studied the case. "Let's try that twenty-two."

Brenda touched Kyle's arm. "Why are we here?"

"You need to know how to handle a gun."

"Why? Isn't that what you're for?" she whispered with a pointed look.

"Just in case."

"Just in case what?" She stared at him in horror. In case he died and she was left to defend herself alone? The thought ripped a wide crevice of fear through her.

He shrugged. "Things happen. Situations can get out of control. I want you prepared."

Swallowing was suddenly hard. "Is this normal procedure? For you to teach your clients to shoot?"

"Sometimes," he said, picking up the small-caliber handgun the store clerk had set on the glass-case top and testing the weight. "This will work. I'll buy a box of ammo."

Heart pounding with adrenaline and a good dose of trepidation, Brenda followed Kyle into the shooting gallery like a sheep being led to slaughter. With each step, her anxiety kicked up, but she couldn't seem to stop herself. Part of her wanted to know how to shoot. Wanted to be capable of defending herself with a firearm if need be. She just hoped the need never came. She wished she had faith like Kyle. Had it in her to pray and ask God for help. She just couldn't quite bring herself to that place.

After she donned the protective eyewear and earphones, Kyle said, "The first thing you have to know is always handle a gun with the thought that it is loaded." His voice sounded muffled through the earphones. "Second, always point the gun away from yourself and away from anyone else. Keep the weapon pointed downrange or down at the ground."

She nodded, staring into his eyes. She didn't want to look at the weapon he was so easily loading.

"Third, always keep your finger off the trigger and outside the trigger guard until you've made the decision to shoot. Fourth, always beware of the target, backstop and beyond. In here it isn't a concern. But out in the real world, a bullet meant for a bad guy could just as easily find its way into an innocent bystander."

With each word, her anxiety ratcheted up. She hoped she'd never have to use a gun in the real world.

"When you hold a gun, a two-handed grip is best. Take your dominant hand and place it high on the backstrap." He positioned his right hand on the back part of the gun. "This gives you more leverage and will help control the recoil.

"Place your support—" he waved his left hand "—so that it is pressed firmly against the exposed portion of the grip not covered by the gun hand. All four fingers of your support hand should be under the trigger guard, with the index finger pressed hard underneath it. Like this."

She stared at his strong, capable hands and wondered how many times he had shot at someone. How many times had his aim been true?

"Got that?" he asked.

She blinked and nodded her head. "I guess so."

With a smile, he set the gun down on the platform in front of them, separating them from the shooting range. Then he took her by the shoulders, spun her so she faced the target—the silhouette of a man.

Moving in close behind her, he nudged her knees. "Stand with your feet shoulder-width apart, knees slightly bent."

Awareness of his hard chest pressed against her back robbed her brain of any coherent thought. It took a second for her to adjust her stance.

"Now, pick up your weapon."

With hands that shook, she lifted the handgun, fitting her palm against the handle but keeping her finger away from the trigger just as he'd demonstrated.

He slid his hands down her arms to cover her hands. Pleasant little tingles spread through her system. Her breath hitched.

"Extend your arms all the way," he said. "This baby has a front sight and a rear-sight notch." He pointed to them with his index finger. "Aim at your target and align the top of the front sight so that it lines up with the top of the rear sight. There should also be equal amounts of empty space on both sides of the front sight. Do you have it sighted?"

She licked her lips then nodded as she gazed down the sight at the target's head.

"Aim for the heart." He lowered her hand slightly.

"Good. When you're ready to shoot, you're going to press on the trigger, not pull. You want as little movement on the sight as possible, and that requires steady pressure on the trigger. Keep pressing all the way to the end. You'll be surprised by the discharge, but that's okay."

She didn't like surprises. "Is it going to hurt?"

He chuckled. "It shouldn't. The recoil might jolt you a bit, but you're strong. You can take it."

His confidence made her want to believe him.

"Take a deep breath and slowly exhale as you apply pressure on the trigger." He nudged her finger onto the trigger mechanism.

She inhaled until her lungs nearly burst. Then curling her finger, she squeezed the trigger; it was slack at first then seemed to catch with resistance. She pressed harder. The weapon fired with a jerk and muted boom. Her arms reverberated with the shock wave of recoil.

She'd fired a gun. A heady sense of exhilaration overwhelmed her. "That was...was..." Words escaped her.

"Awesome?"

Pleased that he knew how she felt, she nodded vigorously. "Yes, awesome!"

Kyle gently took the weapon from her and laid it back on the platform with the barrel facing downrange. "Well done."

He pressed a button on the wall next to them, and the target began sliding toward them. As it got closer, she saw where the bullet had torn through the white part of the paper right of the silhouette's head.

Disappointment subdued the rush of firing a weapon. "I'm not a good shot."

"You hit the paper. That's good for a first time." He sent the target downrange.

"You're just saying so to make me feel better."

"No. I'm telling the truth." He stepped back. "Do it again."

She felt exposed without him covering her hand, his warm chest pressed against her back. Squaring her shoulders, she decided she could do this. She picked up the weapon as he'd taught her, sighted, took a deep breath and, as she slowly exhaled, squeezed the trigger. This time the recoil wasn't as bad, though just as surprising.

Grinning, she laid the gun down. "Can I do it again?"

He grinned back. "Have at it."

When she'd expelled the last shell, she'd finally managed to hit the black part of the target just slightly left of center.

"Good job," Kyle said as they left the shooting range and climbed into the SUV.

"That was surprisingly fun," she exclaimed.

"Didn't I tell you you'd like it?" He headed the vehicle out of the parking lot.

"You did." She sat back, feeling content and empowered. Not that she had a gun to carry, but she now knew how to use one. Just in case. She couldn't stop the little shudder at that thought. "Thank you for taking me shooting."

"You're welcome." At a stoplight, he looked at her and tilted his head, his blue eyes studying her.

"What?" she asked, feeling suddenly self-conscious.

He reached out, but when his hand neared her face, she drew back slightly.

"You have a little gunpowder on your cheek," he said.

Feeling foolish, she froze. The rough pad of his finger brushed across her cheek and lingered, sending little tingles shooting through her like Fourth of July sparklers.

Reflexively her hand came up to wipe at the spot. Their fingers collided.

He drew his hand back and placed it on the steering wheel. She rubbed her fingers together.

Up ahead she saw a big one-stop-shopping superstore. "I'd like to stop there," she said, pointing.

Kyle parked the SUV in a spot near the side of the supersize grocery store's side entrance. When Kyle picked up a small carry basket, she shook her head and grabbed a cart. They'd eaten most of Felicia's stew last night and her food this morning. Brenda filled the cart with supplies for three.

Kyle didn't comment on her purchases, even when she grabbed a one-pound bag of peanut M&M's. If she had to be in seclusion, she was going to have some comfort foods available. Peanut M&M's, mac and cheese, tomato soup and toaster pops. These were the things that would make life bearable over the next few days.

"You sure you haven't forgotten anything?" Kyle asked, eyeing her cart.

"I think I'm ready to check out." She pushed her cart toward the cash register and got in line.

The man in front of her glanced back and then spun around. "Brenda, what a surprise seeing you here."

Brenda blinked. Wariness had her muscles tightening. Kyle stepped closer, their shoulders touching, his hand settling possessively at the small of her back. She was startled by the contact as well as how nice it felt, right up until he slipped a finger into her belt loop—undoubtedly so he could jerk her back out of harm's way if need be. She glanced at him. His strong jaw was set in a firm line, his narrowed-eye gaze trained on the man waiting expectantly for her to respond.

White teeth gleamed against the guy's tan skin. He had light brown hair and brown eyes and wore a polo shirt, white shorts and deck shoes. She tried to place the face. Dredge up a name. But couldn't. Could he be the one trying to kill her? She scooted even closer to Kyle and tried for a polite smile, but she was sure it looked more like a grimace. "I'm sorry, do I know you?"

"Roger Harmon. We met at your parents' home last winter," he said, his initial enthusiasm dimming slightly. "I called you several times but could never reach you."

Ah. Now she remembered. Sunday night fix-up. Roger was a dentist, divorced and belonged to her father's yacht club. She relaxed slightly. There was a reason she didn't have an answering machine at her apartment. She didn't want to be obligated to return calls from men her parents set her up with. The answering service at the hospital knew to pass on only legitimate patient calls.

Silence stretched out. She'd been raised to be polite, so she asked, "What brings you to Winthrop Harbor?"

"Sailing tomorrow in a distance race," he said. "Will you be racing?"

Yearning hit her like a rogue wave. She wanted to be out on the water. "No. No racing this weekend."

"The weatherman says this will be the last good weekend for a while," Roger commented.

"I wish you well in your race, then," Brenda said.

"Sir?" the grocery clerk called.

"It was nice seeing you again," Roger said and moved forward to buy his groceries.

Brenda could feel Kyle's gaze on her as they waited for Roger to finish his purchases and head out the store door. When Brenda went to hand the clerk the money, Kyle covered her hand with his, halting her midair.

"Let me," he said, handing over a credit card.

"You don't have to do that," she said, frowning at him. She was pretty sure buying groceries wasn't in his job description.

"It will be in my expense report," he stated as he took his card back from the clerk. They left the store with their groceries. Once the bags were stowed in the cargo space and they were rolling away from the store, Kyle said, "So you race on a team? Why didn't you mention this before? Maybe one of your teammates has it out for you."

She shook her head. "I don't do teams, so there's no worries there."

"But you do race? Roger asked if you were competing."

"I do. In single-person regattas. I have a sweet Sunfish moored at the Chicago Yacht Club." Sailing had started as a way for her and her father to bond. But sailing had become her passion. A way for her to let off steam.

"Tell me about Roger Harmon. How do you know him?"

Brenda sighed. "I don't really know him. He was just someone Mom and Dad fixed me up with last winter. I only met him the one time."

Kyle lifted an eyebrow as he started the engine. "And he didn't call?"

She made a face. "He probably did. I don't have an answering machine."

"Do your parents fix you up often?"

"Occasionally. They want grandkids," she stated. They also thought she was lonely and a workaholic.

She'd admit to the workaholic charge, but because she spent all of her time at work, in a hospital, with people, how could she be lonely? She didn't have time to be lonely.

Kyle's expression turned thoughtful as he drove. "I'm going to need a list of all the men your parents have tried to fix you up with."

She groaned. "I don't remember them. One uncomfortable dinner was enough, thank you. I'm sure my parents will have names to give you." She cocked her head. "Why? You don't think one of them…"

He shrugged. "Could be. I'll have Detective Lebowitz check 'em out."

"I can't imagine that someone my parents thought highly enough of to introduce to me would want me dead." That just didn't seem plausible. "I think this has to do with the lawsuit. Especially now whoever is doing this is fine with harming other hospital staff."

"Okay. Let's go with that for a moment." He turned down the drive toward the cabin. "What exactly is the suit about?"

"The Hanson family is claiming negligence on my part and that of the hospital killed Mr. Hanson."

"Did it?"

"No. It was a routine procedure. Everything was going perfectly. And then, it wasn't," she said.

He brought the vehicle to a halt. They carried the groceries into the house.

"How can you be sure there was no negligence?" he asked as he unloaded a bag.

She blew out a breath and tucked a pound of chicken in the drawer of the refrigerator. "I've gone over the chart notes, the reports and medical history so many times I can recite them by rote. The lawyers have gone over everything. Dr. Landsem has gone over every detail. There was no negligence. There was no logical reason for the man's death."

"And everything has to be logical for you," he said.

"Yes. Is that so wrong?" She folded the empty bags and put them in the recycle bin.

"Not wrong." He shrugged, his gaze holding hers. "Limiting."

"How so?" she asked, curious how his mind worked.

"By putting everything into neatly ordered boxes of cause and effect, you leave no room for the unexpected, the unexplainable. You miss out on aspects of life that could bring great joy and peace."

"Like God?"

"Like God."

"You sound like my mom and dad," she said.

His eyes twinkled. "I knew I liked them for a reason."

"They are likeable." *Like you.* She let the unspoken thought tumble through her mind.

Needing some air, she headed out the kitchen door. Kyle followed her. She could see the lake through the trees. Desperate for the solace found in the gentle lapping waves, in the expanse of blue water reflecting the orange-and-red glow of the setting sun, she kept walking toward the lake. The temperature had cooled. A slight breeze wafted in the air.

The snap of a branch behind them jolted through her. Sudden fear halted her breath.

In one swift motion, Kyle pulled her against him with an arm wrapped around her waist. He swiveled them around so that his big body shielded her while his free hand reached for his weapon, ready to blast whatever threat came their way.

SEVEN

A dog burst through the underbrush. Without pausing, the canine dashed to the right and disappeared again through the trees.

Melting with relief, Brenda dropped her head against Kyle's chest with a strangled laugh. "Only a dog."

He lifted his finger off the trigger and tucked his weapon back into the small holster at his waist.

"Neighbor's dog. I'll have Felicia call and tell them to keep him on a leash."

"Good idea," she said and forced herself to step away from the security and warmth of his arms.

For a long moment neither spoke. She stared at the lake, letting the peaceful scenery smooth the edges of her fear.

Kyle placed his hands on her shoulders. She jumped. She gave him a nervous smile. "Sorry. A little on edge."

"Understandable." Peering at her with an intensity she found disconcerting, he picked up their conservation. "Have you talked to the Hanson family?"

She sighed as an ache sliced through her heart. "Once, right after his death." She closed her eyes briefly as the memory assailed her. "The hardest part of my job is delivering devastating news like that. It's standard for the operating doctor to inform the family of the outcome of the surgery, good or bad."

"What did you say?"

Her heart squeezed tight as she relived that moment. "I told them what happened and that we tried our best to save him. There wasn't much more I could say."

"But you haven't talked to them since then?"

She shook her head and watched a gull dive into the water for food. "The hospital's attorney said we shouldn't have any contact. It could hurt our case and would make me seem guilty."

His eyebrows drew together. "I don't think showing some empathy would make you seem guilty. Sometimes people just need to know others understand."

"Maybe in a perfect world," she said. "This is not a perfect world."

"Perfection is in the eye of the beholder, yes?"

"I suppose."

"Do you feel guilty?"

She turned to stare at him. She studied his face, liking the sharp angles and straight lines. Handsome, yes, but there was something about this man that drew her to him in a way she'd never experienced before. And that scared and confused her almost as much as someone wanting her dead.

When he arched an eyebrow, she realized she hadn't responded to his question. "I do because I can't explain what happened," she admitted.

"Which pricks your pride?"

Her defenses rose. "It's not pride, it's expectations." Since as far back as she could remember, people expected her to do well; ace her tests, excel at her chosen field and perform flawless surgeries. Be the best, do the best.

"Ah, but whose expectations?"

"Everyone's." The pressure to live up to the expectations placed on her at times seemed overwhelming.

One side of his mouth curved. "Yours included?"

"Yes," she conceded. "I'm expected to be perfect all the time. I have to be."

"No one can be perfect all the time, Brenda," he said, his voice gentle.

Figured she'd get a bodyguard who noticed and dissected stuff. Funny. She was usually the one doing the dissecting. Only she dissected the physical, not the emotional. Life was easier that way. Keeping everyone at an emotional distance allowed her to remain focused on her work. But it also kept her from being hurt. The realization didn't settle well.

She blew out a breath. "What are you? Some armchair psychologist?"

A flash of sadness marched across his face. "No. I could never claim to be that."

Meeting his gaze, her mouth went dry. Her insides turned to mush. He was perfect in an imperfect way that defied logic. Strong, capable, charming, yet irreverent. From the moment he'd walked into Dr. Landsem's office, she hadn't intended to like him. Yet she did.

Attraction sizzled in the air around them, making her yearn for something she had no business wanting. He was her bodyguard. His objective was to keep her alive, not fulfill some latent girlhood fantasies of being rescued by a knight in shining armor.

Okay, so he didn't have on armor. He had on jeans, a T-shirt and canvas shoes, but he'd saved her life. She had to remember not to let the situation go to her head.

* * *

Later that evening, Brenda shooed Felicia out of the kitchen. "I'm making dinner for us."

Delight lit up Felicia's eyes. "You are? How lovely."

A pink hue touched Brenda's cheeks. "I took some cooking lessons last year. I make a mean chicken soup."

"Sounds delicious," Felicia said with a wide smile. "I'll leave you two to it, then."

Kyle leaned against the counter. "You took cooking lessons, huh?"

Brenda set the oven to heat up. "My mother tried to teach me when I was young, but I wasn't much interested. I was too focused on my grades as a kid. But after years of eating out or eating microwavable food, I decided I needed to know how to make a few things just in case—" She opened the refrigerator and pulled out several items.

"Just in case?" he prompted when it seemed she wouldn't continue.

"I ever wanted to entertain." She found a pot, filled it with water and set it to boil on the stove.

"And have you?"

Her mouth pressed into a line for a moment. "No. I haven't."

There was the barest hint of regret in her tone. Was the regret because she hadn't taken the time? He pushed away from the counter. "Tonight you do. What can I do to help?"

She sent him a startled look. "You want to help?"

"Sure. Need anything cut up?" He wiggled his eyebrows. "I'm pretty good with a sharp blade." He didn't tell her he had a butterfly knife strapped to the inside of his left calf.

She blinked then returned his smile. "Good. That makes two of us."

He burst out laughing as one of the region's best surgeons tossed him a plastic bag filled with veggies.

"Okay." She pointed toward the wooden block filled with cutlery. "You can cut up the carrots, celery and mushrooms."

"So why haven't you entertained?" he asked as he set about slicing the vegetables and putting the pieces in a large bowl.

She turned on the faucet to rinse the chicken. "I haven't met anyone outside of my parents that I'm interested in entertaining."

Kyle almost cut off his thumbnail. "*Ever?* Or just in the past few days?" he teased, referring to his unexpected appearance in her life.

She shook her head. "The past few days don't count."

For some reason that pleased him. Maybe she wasn't as immune to his charm as she appeared. Hmm. Interesting. "Come on. You expect me to believe you haven't had anyone in your life to cook for?"

She cocked her head and looked at him. "Why is that so hard to believe?"

"Seriously?" Was she fishing for a compliment? She hadn't struck him as that type. He started chopping the celery.

Pushing at a stray strand of hair with the back of her hand, she said, "Yeah, seriously."

He didn't detect any guile in her dark eyes. "Because you're beautiful, smart. Fearless."

She made a face and returned her focus on cooking. "Right. Get real."

He chuckled. "Okay, maybe not fearless. But definitely brave. You've handled the past few days admirably. No hysterics. Which is a huge plus, believe me."

"Have you had to protect many hysterical females?" Curiosity echoed in her tone.

"My fair share." Careful not to divulge identities, he told her about some of his more colorful assignments as they worked side by side in the small kitchen.

Her laughter filled his heart, making his chest expand as he added a dramatic flair to his tales to keep her laughing. He got a kick out of the way her nose crinkled and her eyes danced with enjoyment.

"Stop," she said, holding a hand to her side. "That can't all be true."

"It totally is."

"You should have been a comedian," she commented as she turned to clean up the mess they'd made.

"My sister would agree with you on that."

Brenda paused. "You have a sister?"

"A twin, actually."

"That must be wonderful." Wistfulness tinged her words. "Where does she live?"

"Kaitlin moved to Boston when I took the job at Trent Associates. She's a librarian."

"You're proud of her," Brenda stated, her chocolate-colored eyes regarding him perceptively.

"I am. When my mom died, Kait turned inward. She didn't speak for the longest time. But she loved books. Still does."

"Must have been hard on you and your father."

His heart ached to remember those days. "I was totally self-absorbed in my own pain. I acted out, taking advantage of the fact that my dad pretty much forgot about me. He was an alcoholic and doted on Kait. It wasn't until later that—"

He cut himself off. What was he doing? He never talked about this stuff. He wasn't one of those touchy-feely kinds of guys. He didn't usually feel the need to open up and let anyone see the pain inside. He'd tried that once four years ago with a woman named Linda Francis. She'd thought she could heal him. She'd been wrong. Her disappointment was more than he could take. He'd decided then it was better to keep things light.

"That what?" she asked.

The concern in her pretty eyes called to something deep inside him. A need to share the burden he carried welled up. He scrubbed a hand over his jaw and resisted the urge to dissemble with a joke. Amazing how that often filled in for him when he was uncomfortable. But he couldn't bring himself to do it again with Brenda.

"I realized what he'd done to Kait." His fingers curled into a ball at his side as old rage roared to life.

Compassion and horror mixed in her expression. "He abused her?"

The words were like a serrated blade slicing through his gut. He wanted to deny it, wanted to rewind the clock and go back. He wanted to protect his twin. Regret and guilt lay heavy on his heart. "Yes. But by the time I learned of it, I was miles away at boot camp and she'd run away."

"She never said anything to you?"

He shook his head. "No. She'd suffered in silence while I was out getting myself in trouble. I should've been at home protecting her."

"Even if she'd told you, what could you have done? You were both just kids."

"Doesn't matter. She's my twin. I should have known. If I'd paid any attention, stuck around the house, he wouldn't have been able to hurt her."

"Where did your sister go? She obviously came back."

"Running away saved her life. She ended up in a shelter. Felicia—" Affection filled his chest. "Aunt Felicia ran the place and took Kait under her wing."

Brenda's eyes widened. "So that's how you know Felicia. Wow, that's…amazing."

"She's amazing. She worked with Kait, got her speaking again. Felicia found out what had happened and called in child protective services. The police took my father into custody. He did jail time."

"That was the right thing for her to do," Brenda said sagely. "When you're in a position of authority, like a doctor, teacher or director of a shelter, and you suspect child abuse, you call CPS. I've had to call on several occasions. Not on cases at the hospital, but patients at the downtown clinic."

Another reason to admire this woman. She always did the right thing. Unlike him. He'd turned his back on his sister when she'd needed him the most. "I'm sure child abuse in all its forms happens more than it's reported."

Brenda nodded. "Unfortunately, I suspect you're right. I can only imagine how traumatic it must have been for your sister, for you both, to lose your mother and then to have your father…"

"It was." Her words brought to mind the situation she faced with her own family. "But losing a parent at any time, for any reason, is traumatic."

Her gaze dropped, but not before he saw the welling of sadness in the dark depths of her eyes. "Yes."

He crossed to her and folded his arms around her, feeling her sorrow and pain acutely. He wanted to offer what comfort he could because he understood her hurt so well. She felt stiff within the circle of his embrace, as if she didn't want to depend on him or anyone else for comfort. "You can't lose hope that your dad will beat his illness."

On an audible exhale she softened, relaxing slightly against him. Her head fit perfectly in the well of his throat and her breath, warm through his cotton shirt, was in time to his. He liked having her in his arms a little too much, but he couldn't find it within himself to let go. She was a client, he reminded himself. He shouldn't be letting things get so personal. Knowing that and acting on it were two different things. Right now, he wanted personal.

"I'm trying not to," she said. "But sometimes hope is hard to find."

Knowing she might refuse, he asked anyway. "Would you like me to pray for him?"

She drew back to look at him, seeming to turn his words over in her head. "I wouldn't mind."

He could see skepticism in the depths of her eyes, but he'd never let that stop him. "Lord, we ask for healing for Brenda's father. We ask for peace and comfort. Amen."

A smile touched the corner of her mouth. "That was short and to the point."

An answering smile curved his lips. "I'm not big on long and drawn out. Usually no time for much more than a 'Help me, Lord.'"

Her expression closed as she stepped out of his embrace. "In your line of work, I can see how that would be true."

She quickly turned to check on the casserole.

Kyle wanted her back in his arms. How crazy was that? Not so crazy, really. They'd shared a moment that went beyond the physical attraction he felt toward her. Heady stuff for sure. But she was the client, and he didn't have any intention of letting either of them become entangled in something that had no hope of going anywhere.

When this assignment was over, when the man wanting to kill Brenda was caught, Kyle would move on to another assignment. That was how it worked. How it had to work. He didn't want anything permanent.

Time to put a little emotional distance between them and concentrate on why they were at the cabin in the first place.

He took out his cell phone. "I'm going to step outside to make a call."

"I'll be right here," she said, her gaze distant now, as if she'd put an invisible wall between them.

He stepped out onto the back porch and moved away from the glow of the porch light. Night had fallen. The outside lights illuminated the backyard and the incline leading to the dock. The moon rose over the horizon and shone brightly on the water's surface. Small gusts of wind rattled through the trees. Kyle called the police and waited for Lebowitz to come to the phone.

"Mr. Martin, has there been another attempt on Dr. Storm's life?"

"No," Kyle was quick to assure the detective. "Where are you in the investigation?"

"Haven't progressed much." Kyle could hear the frustration in the detective's voice. "The crime-scene techs didn't find anything useful at Dr. Storm's apartment or at the hospital. Whoever is behind these attacks is careful."

A professional most probably, then. A hired hit man.

"Have you looked into the family involved in the lawsuit against Dr. Storm?"

"I have. So far nothing to suggest they are the ones trying to hurt the doctor. I've scoured their financials looking for payouts. Nothing."

"Contact her parents." Kyle turned to watch Brenda through the kitchen window. She wiped at the counters with a sponge. "Apparently they've set her up on some 'dates' over the past year. Maybe one of them had their nose bent out of shape when she didn't show interest. One in particular, a Roger Harmon."

Kyle went on to tell him about Roger Harmon showing up in Winthrop Harbor and meeting him at the grocery store. Coincidence? Or something more nefarious? But there was no way for anyone to know where they were or to connect Brenda to Felicia. Or Kyle to Felicia for that matter. Only his boss and sister knew Felicia or where to find her.

"Will do."

"Keep me informed of any developments," Kyle said and hung up.

The fine hairs at the back of his neck prickled as the sensation of being watched swept over him. He spun around. Apprehension slithered down his spine. The presence of an unseen menace whispered to his senses. The threat seeped into his bones.

His gaze searched the surrounding trees, the dark path leading to the water. Was someone out there?

Straining to listen for any telltale signs, he held his breath. The only sound he heard was the slapping of the waves against the dock, the wind sighing through the treetops. Shadows danced in slivers of moonlight. He withdrew his weapon and stepped down the porch stairs into the darkness.

* * *

Brenda wrung out the sponge she'd used to clean the countertops. Her hands used more force than necessary. Water sprayed from the porous fibers and splattered the front of her shirt. She rolled her eyes and tossed the sponge into the sink.

Her head was filled with so much confusion. She couldn't deny her attraction to Kyle or the connection flowing between them. Her heart ached at the pain she heard in his voice as he talked of his past, of his sister. His twin. Their suffering made her want to weep. Which was so unlike her. She normally wasn't overly emotional, didn't cry at sappy commercials and didn't sigh over puppies or babies. Suffering was part of the human condition. As a medical professional, she worked hard to counteract the ravages of disease and age, but she'd never understood or accepted the cruelty that pervaded humanity.

She didn't know how to help Kyle overcome the guilt he carried for what his father had done to his sister. It wasn't right that he should feel that way. But she had no way of helping him. Her specialty ran to the physical, the internal organs, not psychology or emotions.

She wondered how he could cling to his faith. Questions hammered at her.

Where had God been when Kyle's sister was suffering abuse?

Where was God now that her own father's body was being ravaged by disease?

The questions ricocheted off the walls of her brain, making her head ache. To find answers she'd have to admit to believing in God. She supposed she did believe in an abstract way, mostly from her upbringing. But not in a concrete, know-it-in-your-gut kind of way.

She replayed Kyle's prayer in her mind. He'd asked for healing. Peace and comfort. Would God hear the request? Did she dare believe He might?

She spun away from the sink, checked on the casserole again before seeking out Felicia. She found her in the living room, measuring the front window.

Felicia smiled when she saw Brenda. "I was thinking of putting in some wooden blinds over this window to give the room a more rustic feel. What do you think?"

"I think wood blinds would add a lot to the room."

Felicia set the tape measure down. "I'm sorry, I'm being selfish. You have bigger worries than whether I should redecorate."

"You're not selfish at all," Brenda was quick to reassure her. "I appreciate that you're letting us stay here for a few days."

"Kyle said your father is ill. On top of everything else, I can't imagine how worried you must be," Felicia said.

As much as Brenda hated that someone wanted her dead and that two people had already died, the situation had kept her from dwelling too much on her father's sickness. If she weren't hiding out here, she'd be there at his side, whether he wanted her there or not. But staying away for now was what was best. Though being distracted didn't keep the worry from wreaking havoc with her insides.

"It is hard." Brenda tried for a smile, but failed. "Dinner will be ready in a few minutes."

Felicia gave her a hug.

Brenda received the embrace with a wave of longing for her mother.

When Felicia let her go, she said, "I'll go freshen up."

Brenda returned to the kitchen. She took the casserole out of the oven and placed the dish on a wire rack to set. She looked around. Kyle wasn't back. Was he still on the phone?

Or had something happened to him out there? No. She wouldn't let herself think that way. He was capable and strong and would keep them safe.

To busy and calm herself, she set the table and then gathered the trash bag from under the sink. She stepped out the kitchen door. The porch was empty. Kyle was nowhere in sight.

A prickling of unease made her frown. She dismissed it as paranoia. She had every right to be jumpy. She walked down the porch stairs and around the corner of the house to put the trash bag in the big garbage bin.

The stillness of the night was broken by a noise behind her. Terror slammed through her mind and jumpstarted her heart. She whipped around, the trash-can lid clutched in her hand like a shield.

Kyle stepped out of the shadows. Moonlight splashed across his face, lighting up his blue eyes and emphasizing his strong jawline. "Sorry. Didn't mean to scare you."

Lowering the lid, she took a deep breath to still her pounding heart. "Is everything okay?"

"Yes. I've done a perimeter sweep. All clear."

Good to know. "I meant with your call."

"I talked to Lebowitz. Whoever is after you is careful, experienced. They didn't leave any prints or particulates behind."

She didn't like the sound of that: no evidence meant no leads, which meant the investigation might be at a standstill. She fought back a little rise of panic. "What does that mean for the investigation?"

His jaw tightened. "It means we may be dealing with a hired killer."

She flinched as fear grabbed hold of her and squeezed the air from her lungs. "Which means the investigation might be more difficult, given we could be dealing with a professional?"

"Possibly."

She gave him a disbelieving look. "Don't try to minimize this," she said. "I need you to be honest with me."

He canted his head to the side. "All right. I won't try to minimize."

"Thank you."

He stepped closer and put a firm arm around her shoulders. "Focus on the fact that you know I'll do everything in my power to keep you safe."

She wanted to believe him. Needed to believe he'd keep her safe, if she wanted to stay sane and make it through this nightmare.

They reentered the house. Kyle locked the door behind them. They sat down to eat, and she was happy her beginner cooking skills had helped her turn out a better-than-expected meal. And by the contented sighs and nearly empty serving dish, Kyle and Felicia agreed.

"Coffee, anyone?" Brenda asked.

Felicia shook her head. "Not for me. I need to sleep tonight."

"I'll take some," Kyle said.

Brenda rose from the table and moved toward the cupboard.

A loud bang and the sound of metal crashing against metal came from outside, just below the kitchen window.

She froze. Breath-stealing fright invaded her.

Kyle jumped from his seat. "Get down."

Brenda crouched where she was, her heart slamming against her ribs, her breathing turning shallow. Felicia slid off her chair and covered her head with her hands. Kyle flipped off the kitchen lights. With his weapon drawn, he ran out the back door.

Worry that something might happen to Kyle sharpened the fear stabbing at Brenda. A prayer rose unbidden from the depths of her soul. *Please, God, keep him safe.*

EIGHT

Kyle waited for his eyes to adjust to the dark. Without the glow of the porch light, he had only the moon to guide him across the porch and down the stairs. Keeping close to the house, he moved toward the sound of movement coming from around the corner near the garbage cans. He reached inside one of the pockets on his cargo pants and brought out a small Maglite. Steadying his breath, he cleared the corner of the house as he flipped the flashlight on.

Near the toppled garbage cans, two sets of beady eyes glowed brightly behind dark masks.

Raccoons.

Kyle let out a small laugh of relief.

The animals hissed, drawing him away from the sensation of danger raising the fine hairs at the back of his neck.

"Get!" Kyle shooed at them.

The beasts ran away into the shadows.

After cleaning up the mess and making sure the lids on the cans were secure, he headed back inside. He opened the door to the kitchen and flipped on the light. "Everything's okay."

"What was that noise?" Brenda asked, her voice

echoing with alarm. She was sitting with her back against the cupboards, her knees drawn to her chest.

Holding out his hand, he helped her to stand. "Just a couple of raccoons. They'd gotten into the garbage."

She blew out a breathy laugh. "That's a relief. I must not have put the lids on the cans tight enough."

Kyle moved to help Felicia rise from beneath the table. "Pesky nuisances, those raccoons. At least it wasn't a skunk. There have been quite a few in the area lately." Felicia patted his arm. "Glad you're here to protect us." She stepped around him. "I'll finish up the dishes."

"You don't have to do that," Brenda said.

"But I'd like to, dear," Felicia replied over her shoulder. "You cooked. I'll clean."

"Then I'll say good night."

Kyle walked her to her room. A stray strand of dark hair had escaped from her bun and fell across her cheek, making her look fragile. She wasn't. She was tough and brave and kind. He reached up to tuck the strand behind her ear. Her dark eyes flared with a look he recognized as interest, attraction, longing, because he felt it all, too.

Forcing his hand back to his side, he said, "Good night, Brenda. Sleep well."

For a moment, she stared at him as if his words didn't make sense, then she blinked and stepped back. "Good night."

Wide-awake despite the fact she'd made sure the curtains were closed last night, Brenda checked her watch. The face glowed brightly in the dim room. Ten minutes to seven. She'd hoped for another deep, dreamless night of sleep, but no go.

She'd been too keyed up, both by her awareness of

Kyle as a handsome, attractive man and by the fact she'd prayed. Something she hadn't done since she was a young child. She supposed those long-ago Sunday-school lessons had planted seeds of faith in her heart that she wasn't aware of. Kyle's faith had stirred those seeds to life. She didn't know if they'd grow or wither away.

To distract herself from all the confusion messing with her peace of mind, she'd reached for the bag of peanut M&M's and the medical-review magazine she'd bought at the store. At the rate she was going, she'd gain five pounds before the weekend was up. Somewhere in the wee hours of the morning she'd finally drifted off.

She rose and dressed, then made her way down the hall. At the closed door to Kyle's room, she paused. Should she wake him? Probably. Her shadow wouldn't be too happy if she left the house without him. She knocked. Nothing. She knocked again. Still no answer. He must already be up.

She went downstairs and entered the kitchen to find Kyle sitting at the table reading from a Bible. His un-ruly hair was damp, as if he'd recently showered, and his jaw clean shaven. He wore dark cargo pants and a green T-shirt that stretched against his well-defined chest in such a distracting way she forced herself to look at his nose. "Good morning."

"Good morning. You're up early." She smiled as if she were calmer than she was, and then turned to con-centrate on making coffee.

"I hope I didn't disturb you," he said.

If she didn't count how his good looks got to her. "Not at all." She inhaled the aroma of the dark roast coffee filling the pot. She eyed his Bible sitting next to him. "Doing a little light reading?"

"Morning devotional."

She lifted her eyebrows. "Every morning?"

"When I can, but especially on Sunday mornings."

She hadn't realized it was Sunday. Usually she spent the day at the clinic, since it was her official day off at the hospital. She handed him a mug of coffee and then sat down at the table next to him. "You said you didn't grow up with faith, so when did you…find God?"

"One of my buddies in the SEALs was a believer." A sad light entered his eyes. "Chase told me about God, helped me to understand my need for faith. The need to read God's word every day."

The look of grief stealing over him made her heart pound. "Is he…?"

"Dead?" He nodded stiffly. "Yes. He was killed in action."

She ached for him, for the loss of his friend. He must feel as if God betrayed him. "And yet you still believe?"

A slight smile curved his mouth. "You think I should blame God for Chase's death?"

She sipped her coffee, stalling. She didn't know what to think. This was very confusing for her. Her head told her there wasn't a God, but deep in her heart those seeds of faith tugged at her to believe. "Don't you?"

"No. God didn't pull the trigger on the AK-47 that stole Chase's life. An insurgent did that."

She tried to remember more of the lessons she'd learned as a child. "But isn't part of faith believing that God is in control?"

"God is in control." He said it with conviction in his tone.

Anguish welled from deep within her. She only wished having faith was as easy for her as it was for Kyle. "If He's in control, then why did He let your friend die?" Her voice came out harsh, accusatory. "Why does He allow war? Disease?" Her voice cracked on the word.

He set his mug down and reached across the table to engulf her free hand in his much bigger ones. They were warm and callused and electrified, but the compassion flowing through him distracted her and brought tears to her eyes. She blinked rapidly, fighting to hang on to her composure.

"God didn't make your father sick, Brenda," he said gently.

Her heart beat rapidly with hope and skepticism. "Can He heal him?"

"I've no doubt He could. But healing your father may not be God's will."

Not what she wanted to hear. "You said I shouldn't lose hope that God will heal my father. But yet you're saying it might not be God's will to heal him. How can I have hope in God when there's no guarantee He'll do as I want?"

"That's where faith comes in. You have to trust God has a plan. And sometimes that doesn't line up with what we want."

She didn't want her father to suffer, to die. Being a doctor didn't make her immune to heartache. "It's not fair."

"Life's not fair," Kyle stated softly, each word full of pain. "God never promised it would be."

Guilt swamped her. Kyle had lost his mother to disease, too. And yet he didn't blame God. "Could comfort really be found in faith?"

"Yes." Conviction rang in his voice. "Knowing that a loving God cares for me and has a plan for me gives me peace."

She clung to Kyle's hand for a moment as a need

grew within her that she didn't understand. She wanted what he had. She wanted to have peace and comfort and faith.

Brenda slipped her hand away from Kyle's as Felicia entered the kitchen.

"Good morning, my darlings," Felicia said.

Brenda rose. "There's fresh coffee brewed. And I can make some eggs if anyone is interested."

"The smell of coffee lured me out of my bed," Felicia said, taking a mug from the cupboard. "Toast is all I have time for this morning. I'm off to church. Would you two care to join me?"

The thought of going to church grabbed ahold of Brenda. She hadn't set foot in a church since she was twelve, when she'd finally told her parents she didn't want to go anymore. She remembered the hurt on her mother's face, the disapproval in her father's eyes. Her gaze sought Kyle's. "Could we go?"

Surprise brightened the blue of his eyes. "You want to?"

She understood his surprise. She'd made it clear she wasn't sure about God and faith. But the thought of going to church appealed to her this morning. Maybe because of Kyle's steadfast faith or their conversation. Maybe because her father was so ill and she needed something, someone, to give her hope. Maybe because her life seemed so empty right now. "Yes. I would like to. If you think it would be safe for us to."

He contemplated her for a moment. "There's some risk. If someone else recognizes you and word gets out that you're in town, it could lead the killer here."

Anger at this unknown person making her life a living nightmare had her fingers curling. "Running into

Roger was a fluke. I don't know anyone in this town.
How about I wear a hat and glasses?"

"Like a celebrity hiding from the paparazzi," Felicia said.

If only hiding were that simple. But it wasn't. She
couldn't go back into an operating room until her life
was no longer in danger. Brenda waited for Kyle's decision. She trusted Kyle's judgment. She'd come to rely
on her bodyguard. She was afraid that she was also
growing to care for him more than she should, more
than was safe.

Kyle gave a slow nod. "But we sit in back and you
keep a low profile."

"I promise."

They arrived at the small community church on
the edge of town just after the service started. Kyle
led Brenda and Felicia in. He scanned the sanctuary
quickly, noting the exit doors. They found seats in the
very last pew. Brenda sat between Kyle and Felicia. Her
face was well hidden behind the large-brimmed sun
hat and big round glasses she'd donned before leaving
the cabin. Kyle saw a few curious glances from mostly
the women parishioners. They probably did wonder if
some Hollywood figure was sitting in their midsts. He
still had a hard time believing she'd wanted to come to
church. Her attitude had been so rigidly against faith
just a few days ago. But then again, having someone
trying to kill you could put life into perspective. Whatever the case, he hoped she'd find the peace that could
only be found in faith.

An older woman with flame-red hair played a piano
in the corner. The melody rose from the instrument, a
clear and pleasing sound. Taking the hymnal from the

pocket of the back of the seat in front of him, he consulted the program and then turned to the hymn the congregation was singing.

He held it so Brenda could read the words. She sang softly, her voice light and airy. He stopped singing to listen to her.

She nudged him.

He grinned and resumed adding his baritone voice to hers. He liked this, liked being with her, and could easily envision a lifetime of Sunday mornings with her.

Whoa! Where had those thoughts come from?

He didn't want to settle down. He didn't want to be tied to another person. Thinking of Brenda in terms of a lifetime wasn't happening. Not today or any day.

When the music ended, the pastor stepped to the pulpit. Young and charismatic, the pastor read from the first chapter of the book of John. Kyle hadn't realized how starved for the word of God he'd been. Feeling as if his soul was being nourished, he listened while keeping a vigilant eye for anything that could possibly pose a threat to Brenda. At one point he glanced at her. She was listening, really listening. Her expression was intent, her eyes sharp. She was absorbing the words and hopefully the message of God's love for His people.

When the service ended, Kyle hustled the women to the SUV before too many people had vacated the building.

Felicia sighed. "That was lovely. Thank you, Kyle, for taking us."

"You're welcome." He glanced at Brenda.

She smiled. "I'm still taking it in."

"Good enough." Considering how closed off she'd been to faith not that long ago, any progress was welcome.

"I'd like to call my parents again," she said. "They haven't answered the last two times I called."

He handed his cell over.

By the look of concern on her face, they weren't picking up. He made a mental note to call Lebowitz when they returned to the house and have the detective check on them.

When they arrived back at the lake cabin, dark clouds hovered on the horizon. The weatherman's prediction of a storm was proving true. The air grew thicker with humidity. Leaves blowing in the wind swirled in the air.

Kyle opened the front door of the house and stepped inside.

Brenda stepped inside beside him. "Oh, no."

"My house!" Felicia exclaimed.

The place had been ransacked. The cushions of the couch and two armchairs were shredded, as were the curtains that once hung over the windows. Pictures had been taken down and the glass crushed on the floor.

The destruction was similar to that at Brenda's apartment. Like a taunt. The egomaniac after Brenda wanted to make sure they knew they'd been found. No doubt about it, the guy had a personal grudge against Brenda to grind.

Kyle reached for his weapon.

Time to retreat. He hustled the women back to the safety of the SUV. One look at the tires sent his blood jolting through his system.

All four tires had been slashed.

Apprehension climbed on his back and rode him hard. Their intruder was close by, and he wanted Kyle to know it. "Back inside, quick."

Without questioning him, Brenda and Felicia rushed toward the front door. Kyle kept a close watch on the tree line. When they were securely inside, Kyle called 911. The dispatcher said the nearest unit was fifteen minutes out.

Kyle prayed they had fifteen minutes.

"There's someone out there," Kyle said, turning from the window.

The fierce expression on his face made Brenda swallow.

In that moment she saw the warrior, the Navy SEAL expert in underwater demolition.

He wasn't just a thrill seeker, but a man of action. A man who stood between her and certain death. His hand gripped his weapon with ease.

She missed the grin, longed for him to put his arms around her, making her feel safe.

"Upstairs, now!"

His whispered command galvanized Brenda into action. She didn't question him. He was here to protect her, and she trusted him to do just that. She grabbed Felicia's arm and ran for the stairs with Kyle right behind them.

As they hit the top stair, the sound of breaking glass sent shards of panic along Brenda's nerve endings.

"To the back bedroom," Kyle said, his voice low, urging them forward. He pushed the door open. "Inside. Lock the door and don't open it until I tell you."

"What are you going to do?" she asked, reluctant to let him face this threat alone. They were dealing with a killer; two people had already died. She didn't want him to be a third. "Stay with us."

He ran a knuckle down her cheek. His sudden tenderness, the way his whole body gentled, rocked her.

"I'll be right outside this door. No one's getting to you without going through me first."

A fresh wave of panic washed over her. He'd die protecting them. The thought filled her with a deep anguish that felt like a physical blow. "That's what I'm afraid of."

His eyes widened slightly. Then he grinned. "Don't worry. I can handle this."

"But what if…" Tears burned her eyes. His death would be another burden for her to carry.

He pressed a finger lightly to her lips. "Shhhh. Trust me. And say a quick prayer."

Pressing her lips together to keep from begging him not to leave, she nodded. *Please, God, keep him safe.*

He stepped back, pulling the door closed with him. Brenda's heart squeezed tight. If anything happened to him…

Felicia put her arm around Brenda's shoulder. "He'll be fine. This is what he's good at."

She told herself Felicia was right. He was a SEAL, trained to take out bad guys. But even knowing that couldn't stop the terror from invading her mind and her heart. In such a short span of time, she'd come to rely on him in a way she'd never done with anyone else. He'd become dear to her. Stunned, she realized her heart had become involved. And she didn't know what to do about it.

"You care for him," Felicia stated softly.

"Yes," she admitted quietly. Cared. Such a simple and generic word. Caring meant friendship, mutual enjoyment of each other's company. Caring meant she didn't want anything bad to happen to him. All true.

But she couldn't let herself go beyond caring. He was a temporary fixture in her life. She had a job she longed to return to. Having deeper feelings for her bodyguard would only lead to heartache. She had enough of that going on right now with her father's diagnosis to voluntarily ask for more. As much as she liked and cared for Kyle, she couldn't let her heart become any more attached, because it would hurt too much when he left. And leave he would.

Her life was in Chicago. His wasn't. End of story.

As minutes ticked by, her anxiety grew, compelling her to search the room for something, anything, for her and Felicia to defend themselves with. Where was Kyle? Was he just outside the door, or had he gone hunting for the intruder? Or was he lying somewhere in the house, hurting and possibly dying while a madman searched for her?

She yanked a brass table lamp off the bedside stand and tested its weight. She could do some damage with this. But it wouldn't stop a bullet.

The sound of sirens announcing the arrival of the police brought welcome relief. Both from the fear lodged in her throat like a rock and the thoughts of Kyle hurt tying her insides up in knots.

A knock on the door jump-started her heart.

"It's safe. You can unlock the door," Kyle said.

Hearing Kyle's voice eased the lump of dread from her throat. She unlocked the door and pulled it open. Kyle stood there, unharmed, with that cocky smile she was beginning to grow used to.

She fought the need to touch his face and prove to herself he was okay. Her stomach clenched, and the urge to fly into his arms and cling to him in relief welled. It took every ounce of control she possessed to resist.

Wrapping her arms around her middle and firmly tucking her hands away, she asked, "What happened?"

"Guy bolted when he heard the siren."

"Did you see him? What did he look like?" Brenda asked, still reeling that they'd been found.

"He was dressed all in black. Didn't get a look at his face." He held out his hand. "Time to roll."

Slipping her hand into his, she felt the strength in his grip and hoped like crazy that her heart would have as much strength to resist the allure of her bodyguard. Because if she didn't, the eventual heartache would cut her to the quick.

A cut she wasn't sure she'd recover from.

NINE

"Here we go," Kyle said, pushing open the door to the hotel room he'd just secured for the night while they waited for Trent Associates to secure a safe house.

After leaving the cabin in Winthrop Harbor, Kyle had made arrangements for Felicia to fly to Boston to visit Kaitlin. He wanted Felicia out of harm's way.

He'd tried to talk Brenda into a trip to Massachusetts as well, but that suggestion went over like a lead balloon. The woman stubbornly refused to travel far from Chicago in case her father's condition worsened. She wanted to be here for him and her mother.

Kyle didn't blame her. He'd have felt the same if it were his sister who was ill.

Brenda squeezed past him to enter the hotel room. The scent of her lightly floral perfume filled his head, making him want to nuzzle her slim, graceful neck. She stopped in the middle of the room near the king-size bed and turned around to pin him with a quizzical look. "Where are you staying?"

He grinned. "Nothing gets past you, does it?"

She arched an eyebrow. He moved to open the connecting door and then tapped on the closed connector to the next room. "I'll be in here."

Visibly relaxing, she set her shopping bag with her clothes and toiletries on the bed. "Now what?"

"Rest."

"I'd rather go see my father," she said, worry clouding her eyes.

Lebowitz had called with the news that Mr. Storm had been admitted to the hospital with pneumonia. The detective had assigned a guard for Brenda's father as a precaution.

Kyle shook his head. "No can do. I'm not letting you anywhere near Heritage Hospital until this maniac is caught." There were too many variables he couldn't control. Too much at stake. He couldn't let anything happen to her. If he were honest with himself, his reasons had more to do with how much he cared for her than the fact she was his protectee.

"Dad's not at Heritage," she pointed out. "He's at Chicago Memorial, which should be safe, right? You said Detective Lebowitz has guards posted at his door. If he's safe, then I'd be safe."

Her hopeful tone affected him more than he wanted to admit. He didn't want to take chances with her life, but she made a good point. There were guards on-site; the place had more security, lots of cameras. And hopefully, their bad guy wouldn't have access the way he did at Heritage. "I'll call Chicago Memorial in the morning and talk to their security department. If we can work out some reasonable security measures, we'll go."

A soft smiled played at the corners of Brenda's mouth. "Thank you."

The need and vulnerability in her eyes, on her face, shot straight to Kyle's heart. He didn't question himself when he took two long strides to her side and gathered her close to his chest. He normally didn't get so personally invested with his protectees. Keeping an emotional distance usually wasn't a hard thing for him. Sure, he'd remained friends with a few of his past assignments. But holding Brenda so close, feeling her arms wrapped around his waist, her small, yet strong hands on his back, felt like more than friendship. The longing to kiss her had him tightening his hold.

His mind warred with his heart.

Be a professional, his mind advised, but his heart wanted nothing more than to give in to the affection and attraction filling his chest.

This is a dangerous road, his head reminded him.

You live for danger, his heart shot back.

Don't go making promises you can't keep, his mind cautioned. His heart didn't have an answer to that.

You are not her future. His mind and his heart were in agreement there.

Time to beat feet and regroup. Because the last thing he'd ever want to do was hurt Brenda by leading her to believe he and she…they could ever be a couple.

He loosened his hold and eased her away from him.

Her brown eyes, so full of trust and something else that made his heart stammer, searched his face, looking for something he couldn't give her. It was better to ignore what was building between them. For both their sakes.

"I'll be right next door if you need anything," he said.

With a nod, she stepped back, increasing the distance between them. "I'll knock if I need you."

"You *scream* if you need me," he said. "Keep the connecting door ajar."

"I will."

He left her room and entered the room next door. He cracked open the connecting door, gratified and disconcerted at the same time to see she'd left the connecting door to her room wide open. So like her heart. He doubted she even realized how open she'd become over the past few days. All the sharp edges were a defense mechanism to safeguard the soft, wonderful woman inside. A woman he knew deserved so much better than a man like him.

The next morning, after talking with Chicago Memorial's security staff and arranging for extra guards, Kyle escorted Brenda to see her father on the sixth floor. The room was small and consisted of a bed, a wall-mounted TV and a cart with supplies. Her father lay in the bed with an IV and tubes running in and out of his body. As Brenda went to her father's side, Kyle marveled at her composure.

Her father didn't look so good. And Kyle could see the toll it was taking on Brenda by the lines of worry bracketing her eyes and pinching the corners of her lush mouth. But she remained poised and calm. Focused.

Must be a doctor thing, because Kyle was struggling and the man lying in the bed wasn't even related to him.

Suddenly, visions of another hospital room flashed jaggedly in his mind. He heard the soft beeping sound of the monitors, the smell of antiseptic, the nondescript walls. All those horrible memories served to transport Kyle back in time to when his mother was sick.

His stomach pitched, and vague nausea welled. He wanted to turn around and run out the door. He didn't. He couldn't. Brenda needed him.

Or rather, his client. He couldn't let himself forget the nature of their relationship, no matter how much a part of him wished it were otherwise.

He wasn't a part of this family. He was an outsider,

so staying back, out of the way, was the professional thing to do. He took a position near the door. Hospital security would patrol the corridor, and Lebowitz would keep a cruiser in the area. Still, he kept an alert vigil.

All the necessary precautions had been made to ensure Brenda's safety; he'd done all he could, had put every ounce of himself into protecting her. But that didn't mean she wouldn't be hurt, even if he didn't believe anybody could ever be one hundred percent safe. He'd seen too much to ever have complete peace of mind or to let complacency take root.

But he had a sinking feeling as he watched her hovering over her father that the hurt she would most likely experience would be more damaging than a physical blow.

He wanted to protect her physically *and* emotionally. And he wanted to be the one to comfort her in her time of need, wanted to be by her side and help her through the difficult days to come.

He wanted to be more than her bodyguard, more than just the guy shadowing her because it was his job to do so.

Talk about losing his composure. Losing focus. These kinds of thoughts could get them both killed.

The sickly pallor of her father's face made Brenda's stomach churn. She'd recognized the look, seen it in patients. But every fiber of her being wanted to deny this was her father. He'd always been a larger-than-life type of guy. She never would have thought she'd see him laid low by anything.

Dark circles beneath his eyes twisted her up inside. A pervading helplessness seeped in. Grief jammed her breath in her throat so that she couldn't even form words.

She checked his chart and approved of the doctor's use of medication. The heart monitor showed a good rhythm. His blood pressure was a little low but acceptable. She fluffed her dad's pillows. Adjusted his covers. Poured him some water. Anything to keep her hands busy and her mind from breaking down. Seeing him in the hospital was so much worse than seeing him ill at home. Here, in her own territory, his sickness seemed so much more real, so much more difficult to handle because she knew what he faced, understood the complexities of his disease and the treatments available. Treatments that may or may not help.

God has a plan. The words rang inside her head as clearly as if Kyle had spoken them. She glanced at him where he stood by the door. His jaw was set, his hands clasped behind his back, his feet braced apart. He made an imposing figure. Her bodyguard. Her heart did a little fluttering in her chest. And her breathing eased a bit.

Lord, I want to trust You have a plan. She sent the silent words heavenward. Of course she meant with her father, but a little part of her wondered what plan God had for her. For her and Kyle.

"Stop fussing, Brendy," Dad said.

She paused, bringing her focus back to her father. He hadn't called her by that nickname for several years. Guilt for once upon a time yelling at him to never call her that ridiculous name clogged her throat. She was thankful to hear him say her name, period.

She gave him a tender smile and managed to ask, "Can I get you anything, Dad?"

His expression softened. "No. I won't be here long. Once the antibiotics kick in, I'll be good as new."

The doctor in her knew the truth, but she didn't want

to argue that point. She didn't want to douse his hope. "Where's Mom?"

"She's at her Bible study. I figure the ladies are probably praying for me as we speak."

Brenda's smile widened. "I'm sure they are." After a heartbeat, she added, "I went to church yesterday with Kyle." She knew he'd appreciate knowing that.

His eyebrows rose and gladness entered into his dark eyes. "I'm glad, Brenda. It's times like this we need to cling to our faith."

Normally, Brenda physically recoiled if her father said such things. Her logical side would discount his faith. But not today. Today she simply accepted her father's belief in God and didn't judge its validity. She glanced at Kyle, knowing he was responsible for her change in perspective. He met her gaze with a level look that sent her pulse skipping. She nodded slightly, answering his unspoken question. Yes, she had faith. He rewarded her with one of his breath-stealing grins. She went all gooey inside.

"Have they caught the person trying to hurt you?"

Her father's question brought her attention back to him and slammed the situation home. As safe as she felt at the moment, she wasn't. Somewhere out there someone wanted her dead. And anyone who got in the way would pay the price. Two people already had. She prayed there wouldn't be a third.

"No," she answered, forcing her voice to stay even. "The police are working on it." She didn't want to tell him about the intruder at the cabin. It would only upset him.

"Where are you staying?"

"We're in a hotel near Navy Pier."

"Is it safe there?"

Kyle stepped forward to answer. "It's safe for now. But I'm picky about her safety, so I'd like to get her out of the state." He turned a stony look her way. "But she refuses."

Dad turned his dark eyes on her. "Brenda, you do as Mr. Martin says. It's in your best interest."

"I know, Dad." Her usually reliable bedside composure slipped and she took an emotional stumble. A bad one. Her eyes welled. A tear rolled down her cheek. Then another. "I'm trying. But I'm not going anywhere far away while you're so sick."

Tears welled in her father's eyes. Surprise siphoned the oxygen from Brenda's lungs. She'd never seen her father cry. She clasped his hand and held on tight.

"Then take *The Bella* out," he said, his voice thick with emotion. "You'd be safe in the middle of the lake and yet close enough to come back if the need arises."

Stunned, Brenda drew in a quick breath. Her dad, who'd never let her take the boat out without him before, was offering up his prized possession...his pride and joy. *The Bella* was a sweet two-cabin vessel that could easily do six knots yet was so comfortable Brenda always forgot she was on the water. She swiped at her cheeks as surreptitiously as she could. "That's generous of you, Dad."

"The Bella?" Kyle asked.

"A Beneteau 311 sailing yacht," her dad answered with pride. "She's a beauty. Brenda knows how to run her."

Brenda met Kyle's gaze. She could see his mind working. He gave a slow nod. "That would work."

"Good. It's settled," her dad said. "Now if you two don't mind, I'm finding it difficult to keep my eyes open."

Knowing she should be affronted that the two men would decide her fate between them without consulting her, Brenda couldn't quite dredge up any anger. Instead, she bent to kiss her father's cheek. His skin felt cold against her lips. "You're cold. I'll get you another blanket."

"That would be nice," he replied as his eyelids drifted closed.

"We'll tell the nurse on the way out," she promised, though she didn't think he heard her. He seemed to have fallen asleep already. A pang tugged at her heart. She and Kyle slipped out of the room. At the nurses' station, Brenda stopped to talk to the woman at the desk while Kyle went to the elevator.

"My father would like another blanket," Brenda told the nurse, whose name tag read Vera. "And if anything happens or you need to reach me, I have my pager." She gave the woman her number.

"Will do, Dr. Storm," Vera said.

Satisfied, Brenda joined Kyle at the elevator. He drew her to the side as the doors slid open. The car was empty. They stepped inside. The doors closed with a soft swoosh.

In the reflection on the stainless-steel door, Brenda noted how much taller Kyle was than her. He held himself with a straight spine, legs braced apart, hands down by his sides. She could feel the restrained energy coiled inside him like heat from a fireplace in winter. Though he had both feet firmly planted, she had no doubt he was primed to spring into action should a threat present itself. She supposed that came with his military training. She could only imagine the battles he'd fought, the fights he'd survived. His body reflected hard work and time spent building muscles not gained in a gym. A warrior.

He caught her gaze in the reflection. His blue eyes sparkled and one side of his mouth quirked. She'd been staring. She held his gaze, though she could feel a blush working its way up her neck.

The door opened, breaking the eye contact between them. He stepped out of the elevator car first, and then motioned her forward. As they walked out of the hospital his hand settled at the small of her back and sent jolts of awareness zinging up her spine. The heat she felt infusing her had nothing to do with the humidity hanging in the air and everything to do with the man at her side.

Unnerved by her reaction, she wasn't aware they'd veered off the main walkway leading to the parking structure until Kyle said, "When I say go, run as fast as you can."

"Wait. What?" she stuttered, trying to understand, but managed to put one foot in front of the other. Kyle didn't answer. Anxiety kicked up a storm of nerves in her belly. Her breath hitched. She braced herself, fearing an attack of some sort.

He gave her a shove. "Go!"

She ran, aware of Kyle at her side, and then he put on the brakes and whirled around. She neared the end of the path. A garden lay before her. Flowers and greenery and benches scattered throughout provided a peaceful place for those waiting for loved ones to sit and find some comfort. If only that were the case now. Not sure what to do, which direction to take, she glanced back.

Fear exploded as she watched Kyle launch himself at a man dressed in black wearing a black hoodie pulled over his head and dark glasses.

Her heart rate quadrupled.

Frozen with fright, she could only stare as the men grappled, each working to gain the advantage.

It was then Brenda noticed the man held something black in his hand. He brought the device up and pressed it to Kyle's side.

Brenda's feet were moving even before the scream tore from her. "Kyle, watch out!"

Kyle heard the pop then two hot barbs hit his side. He'd seen the Taser, instantly recognizing the X26 model as he'd tackled the man following them. Stinging pain jolted through his system.

His abdomen muscle flexed.

He let out a roar.

Someone ran up from behind him. He felt hands on his back going for his weapon.

His attacker rolled away and jumped to his feet.

Jerking from the electric current humming along his nerve endings, Kyle stared in horror as Brenda faced the attacker, Kyle's SIG clutched in her shaking hands.

No! Kyle screamed inside his head.

She sighted down the barrel at the man as Kyle had taught her and squeezed the trigger. She jerked from the recoil.

The bullet hit the man in the shoulder. The assailant cried out and spun but didn't drop. Clutching his shoulder, he fled the scene, his tennis shoes thwacking against the pavement.

Soft hands touched Kyle's face. Brenda knelt beside him. She'd laid his weapon on the ground. "Kyle! Are you all right?"

He lay his head on the cement. He drew in a ragged breath. "No, can't say that I am."

"I'm going to remove the darts," she said, her skilled hands going to work. With a quick, forceful yank, she ripped his shirt at the seam and flipped it back away from the barbs sticking out of his side. She cupped the skin surrounding one electrode with one hand, stretching the skin, and grabbed the tip of the barb with the other hand to yank it straight up and out of his flesh. With quick efficiency, she repeated the process with the second barb. He hissed as fresh bouts of pain momentarily burned through him.

When he could speak again, he said, "Good shot, Brenda."

"I had an excellent teacher," she replied with a wobbly smile.

Gingerly, he lifted the edge of his shirt. Twin red dents appeared in his flesh.

"Let me see," Brenda insisted, batting his hand away when he went to probe around the marks. "Didn't hit your ribs or break the skin."

Kyle tried to ignore the gentle way her hands and gaze touched his side. His skin flamed at every point of contact. If she didn't stop the sweet torture, he'd incinerate.

The sound of police sirens filled the air. Obviously someone had called the cops. Good. Saved him the effort.

"Tasers are a nonbloody way of taking down an opponent," he commented through his teeth.

She let her hands drop away from him, much to his relief and disappointment. "It didn't stop you," she said.

A crowd had gathered. They were vulnerable out here in the open. He needed to get Brenda aboard her dad's yacht ASAP.

He sat up and forced his legs beneath him. Brenda

wrapped an arm around his waist, offering her support. He doubted she'd be able to hold him up if he started to go down, but the thoughtful gesture sent affection unfurling through him.

"That's 'cause I'm invincible," he quipped.

He'd been blessed was more like it. If the guy had had a gun and not a Taser, Kyle could have been a goner. Kyle was going to have Trent send some body armor his way.

Her gaze whipped to his face. "No, you're not invincible. No one is. You could have been killed if…" Her mouth pressed together and she stepped back.

He cocked his head, missing having her soothing fingers on his skin, her supportive arm around his waist. "Is that concern I hear?"

And if it was, was it for him as a patient or for him as a man? Which did he want it to be? His heart clamored to answer. His brain locked out any response. He wasn't her patient, nor was he her man. He was her bodyguard. Period.

"Of course I'm concerned," she snapped. "If you're dead then who's going to protect me?"

"Ah, it's all about you, then."

To his amusement, she sputtered in outrage. "No, of course not. I just mean, you're supposed to be protecting me. You can't do that if you get yourself killed. You have to be more careful."

She protested too much. But this wasn't the time to press her, not after seeing her father and then the attack. "No worries. I don't think God is finished with me yet. I'm sure He has some refining on me left to do," he said. "Besides, I had you as backup."

He still couldn't get over seeing her shooting the bad guy. Admiration for her quick thinking and equally quick action wrapped around his heart, making the feelings he'd been trying to suppress expand until he thought he might burst.

She opened her mouth to reply, but was cut off by an invasion of law enforcement. Uniformed officers took their statements. Crime-scene technicians combed the area, putting up yellow caution tape and marking the blood trail left behind by the assailant with small orange, numbered cones. A few minutes later Detective Lebowitz arrived. Kyle explained what had happened.

Lebowitz turned to Brenda. "Had you ever seen the assailant before?"

"I couldn't really tell what he looked like. He had on a hoodie tied tight around his face so I couldn't see his hair color, and he had on dark glasses that covered most of his face."

"What about you, Mr. Martin? Notice anything that could help identify the assailant?"

"He was scrappy, wiry. Knew how to use aikido."

"That's more than we knew about him a few hours ago," Lebowitz stated. "I'll have all the aikido dojos in town checked out. See if we can find some connection to Dr. Storm. We'll also alert all the hospitals and medical clinics. He'll have to go somewhere to have the bullet wound looked at."

"Detective." A crime-scene technician held out his gloved hand, revealing small disks printed with numbers. "From the Taser."

"What are those?" Brenda asked.

Kyle smiled grimly. "The serial numbers on these pieces of confetti will tell the police where the Taser was sold and hopefully reveal the name of the purchaser."

"That's amazing," Brenda said.

"It's brilliant is what it is," Kyle stated. "Too bad guns and knives don't emit some sort of tracking device to be left at a crime scene."

Brenda nodded. "How did he find us?"

Kyle had been asking himself that same question. "We weren't followed here." He was certain of it. But then he'd been certain they hadn't been followed to Felicia's, either. Had the guy planted a tracker on the SUV? Time for a new set of wheels.

"Are my dad and mom in danger?" Brenda asked in a voice full of anxiety.

"I'll personally make sure they have continued police protection, Dr. Storm," Lebowitz said. "I have a guard outside your father's room."

"You have to find this maniac," Brenda said, her voice shaking with fury and fear. "I can't live like this. My parents shouldn't have to live like this."

Kyle covered her fisted hand with his as empathy knotted his chest.

Sympathy played in Lebowitz's hazel eyes. "I know how hard this is, Dr. Storm. But you have to be patient. We'll get the guy. In the meantime, you have Mr. Martin. He won't let anything happen to you. He's a Bronze Star recipient, making me think he's good at what he does. I'll be in touch." With that Lebowitz walked away.

Obviously the detective had been doing some research on him. Kyle would have been surprised if he hadn't. An embarrassed sort of pride knotted his chest as Brenda turned her curious, wide eyes on him. He didn't need her looking at him as if he was a hero. He'd been doing what he'd been trained to do. What any one of the men in his unit would have done. It just happened to be him who had pulled his CO and two others out of an inferno. No big deal.

"Really? A Bronze Star? For what?"

He gave her a slow grin. "That's classified. If I told you, I'd have to—"

She made a face. "I know. Kill me. That's pretty cliché."

He arched an eyebrow. "I was going to say I'd have to kiss you."

TEN

I'd have to kiss you.

Kiss me indeed, Brenda thought, tightening her hold on the tiller.

She slanted a glance toward Kyle as his words reverberated around her head in time with the vibration of the boat motor as she maneuvered *The Bella* out of the harbor and through the rougher waters of Lake Michigan.

He sat with his legs stretched out in front of him on the starboard side, his back leaning against the railing. He didn't seem to mind the spray of water or the wind tousling his blond hair. He looked relaxed, causal even.

Not like a man who'd just been zapped by a Taser.

Her stomach clenched at the memory of the red, angry sites where the Taser's darts had dug into his flesh.

When she'd been inspecting the wounds, she'd noticed two harrowing-looking scars. The round puckering of a healed bullet wound and the jagged slash of raised skin that could have come only from a blade.

Empathy tightened her chest. She'd wanted to ask about the scars, but she knew him well enough now to know he'd only deflect with some smart-alecky remark. Or accuse her of flirting.

She didn't flirt. Or rather she never had before.

But with him...

As if feeling her gaze, his head turned her way. His blue eyes collided with hers.

I'd have to kiss you.

She couldn't help the tingle of excitement the very idea sent sliding through her. It had been a long time since she'd been kissed. Since she'd even wanted to be kissed. And now that he'd planted the idea in her head, it was all she could think about.

Like a girl not ready for the grown-up challenges she'd impulsively taken on, she panicked and looked away, pretending to check the rigging above his head.

What would it be like to be kissed by him? Would he be tender and giving, or passionate and demanding? The thought made her feel reckless and wild.

Just as being out on the lake made her feel free. And safe. She planned to drop anchor about three miles offshore. Close enough to make land quickly if needed. But far enough out to have a buffer of water between her and danger. Humidity thickened. In the distance, dark gray clouds brought the threat of the first fall storm, but that didn't deter her from her goal. After the past few days, a little weather wasn't going to keep her trapped on land with a madman waiting to kill her.

She forced her gaze forward. They sailed out of the harbor boundary. Heading the bow into the wind, she placed the motor into Neutral then clipped the halyard to the head of the mainsail. Releasing the boom vang, she hoisted the mainsail. The sound of the white polytarp sheet filling with wind was music to her ears.

Unbidden, Kyle fastened the main halyard line to a cleat, saving her the effort. Surprised he knew what to do, she nodded her thanks and cut the engine on the motor. The boat heeled leeward. She quickly worked to raise the jib. Once again Kyle lent his strength to secure the jib halyard and cleated off the line.

A job she normally performed while her father captained the boat. Would she ever sail with him again? Sadness washed over her. But she refused to give in to the pain. She needed to believe her father had time left. Time enough for them to take the boat out on the water again.

Back at the tiller, she turned the boat out of the eye of the wind. The sails grew taut, and they cut through the waves. Water sprayed on deck.

A sense of freedom wrapped around Brenda. Out here she could just be. No pressure to perform. Bad men with guns were far away. Out here she was safe. She caught the grin on Kyle's face, the joy in his blue eyes. He felt it, too. He met her gaze. She smiled. He was a kindred spirit.

Time seemed to stand still and speed up all at once.

Aware of something happening between them, of the connection being forged, Brenda breathed deep, filling her lungs with fresh air and letting herself admit to the attraction, the affection she felt for her bodyguard.

Kyle Martin had caught her off guard. She'd never expected to like, let alone care for, her bodyguard. She respected and admired him. Trusted him with her life. Wanted to be more to him than a client.

But admitting the emotions didn't mean she would do anything about the feelings bouncing around her head and her heart.

Out of self-preservation, she broke eye contact and shifted her gaze to the shoreline. Gauging they were at the point she'd charted on the nautical map, she released the sails, letting the vessel's windage and motion provide the necessary backward propulsion. The boat bounced slightly on the gentle swells. Kyle lowered the anchor from the bow and fed out the anchor line, expertly snubbing it to the bollard along the craft. She stowed the sail and secured it with tie straps.

Only the sound of waves lapping at the hull and the occasional squawk of a seagull broke the silence.

"We did it," Kyle said, making his way aft and resuming his seat.

She leaned against the wheel. "I didn't know you knew how to sail."

His grin was cheeky and made her toes curl inside her canvas deck shoes. "There's a great deal you don't know about me."

But she wanted to know. She wanted to know everything there was to know about this man who'd sliced through her well-constructed reserve and found the tender underbelly of her heart, making her want things in life she hadn't allowed herself to want in such a very long time.

He leaned back and shut his eyes. "It's so peaceful."

"I love it out here," she admitted. Loved looking at him, too.

His eyes opened, the blue seeming even bluer. "It's a nice boat."

Another stab of sorrow shot through her. "Dad's baby."

Tilting his head, he asked, "Did you learn to sail on this craft?"

"No." She moved to sit on the bench opposite him. It felt good to sit, to relax. "He had a different boat then. A small sloop."

"Easier to learn on, I'd imagine."

"Yes." She yawned, realizing how tired she was. She

hadn't slept well the past few nights because of the fear, the worry and the man only a few feet away. Covering her mouth with her hand in embarrassment, she said, "Excuse me."

"No need for excuses. You've had a rough few days," Kyle said as he reached across the space between them to put his hands over hers. "You go below and rest."

His touch sent an electric current running up her arm. She held on tight. Yearnings flooded her senses. She wanted him to pull her into his arms. She wanted to feel the beat of his heart against her cheek as she lay her head against the solid strength of his chest. She wanted to lift her mouth to his...

Shaken by her longings, she forced herself to breathe and extracted her hands. Needing some space, she nodded. "Thanks."

She quickly made her way below deck. Though everything inside of her wanted to go back to him, to ask him to hold her, to kiss her. She halted in the main saloon and pushed aside thoughts of Kyle. Instead, she focused on her surroundings. The gleaming teak and soothing blue crushed-velvet cushions made her smile. She remembered the first time she'd seen the boat after her father refurbished it. She'd teased him that it looked like a bachelor pad. He'd laughed, claiming her mom picked out the interior.

Brenda headed to the forward berth, her parents' space, and lay on the bed, snuggling beneath the down comforter. The scent of her father's aftershave lingered on the pillow. The comfort cocooning her in warmth was tempered with fear and worry.

When would this nightmare end?

And when it did and if she survived, what then?

She'd go back to her life. And Kyle would go back to his. That was the way it was, the way it had to be.

But the future never before looked so bleak.

Night fell, and with it the temperature. Kyle sought warmth and food below deck. The galley was well stocked with canned and dry goods. Trying not to make much noise that would disturb Brenda, he prepared their supper. A can of chili, a box of corn-bread mix that needed only oil and water. He heard the berth door open. He turned and Brenda stepped out. Her dark hair was mussed, her clothes wrinkled. She looked adorable as she blinked at him.

"What are you doing?" she asked on a yawn.

"Making dinner. Your parents keep the cupboards nicely stocked."

"Can I help?"

His answer stalled when she started to finger-comb her hair. The mass spilled about her shoulders, and he had to fight the urge to run his fingers through the silken strands to see if they were as soft as they looked. He liked knowing there was this side of Brenda. So unlike the uptight, in-control surgeon he'd met a few days ago.

He flexed his fingers around the soup ladle, stirring the chili to get a grip. "You could set the table."

She set about the task, and maneuvering in the tight quarters made Kyle acutely aware of Brenda's soft curves every time he bumped into her. It was a relief when they finally sat down to their meal, because he didn't know how much more he could take before he pulled her into his arms and kissed her.

"Can I ask you something?"

"Of course." Curious, he waited while she seemed to gather her thoughts.

"Earlier today you said something about God refining you. What did you mean by that?"

Surprised and glad that she'd feel comfortable enough and curious enough to ask about spiritual matters, he set his spoon down and formed his words carefully. "I was referring to Proverbs 17:3. 'The refining pot is for silver and the furnace for gold, but the Lord tests the heart,'" he quoted.

Her eyebrows knitted together. "Tests the heart?"

"Not a pass-or-fail kind of test, but just as precious metals must be purified by heat, so do our hearts. God uses adversity to shape, mold and purify. To get rid of the dross and to prepare us for great blessing or great suffering." He wasn't sure how to make her understand. "It's kind of a hard thing to explain. I'll admit it took studying the Bible to really grasp the analogies."

"I kind of get what you're saying," she said, her intelligent gaze thoughtful. "Silver has to be mined, then refined through a labor-intensive process, requiring time, patience, attention and care before it can become something precious and worthwhile. Something beautiful."

A warm smile spread through him. "Exactly."

Her mouth curved up in an almost shy smile. "I did go to Sunday school as a kid. I haven't forgotten everything."

His heart swelled and he reached across the expanse of the table to touch her hand. She was so beautiful. Smart, kind and caring. A woman worth loving.

Stunned by that conclusion, a humming sounded in his brain, and the world tilted.

Wait. That wasn't an imagined sound.

His pulse skyrocketed.

Shoving his shocking thought aside, he cocked his head and listened. He'd heard an out-of-place noise. "Did you hear that?"

"What?"

Heavy footsteps echoed in the main cabin like the blast of a gun. He had heard the whir of a motor. Someone was on the deck. His senses went to full-combat mode.

The alarm on Brenda's face made his stomach clench. He grabbed his weapon from a drawer where he'd stashed it earlier. "Get in the cabin. Lock the door. Do not come out."

She scrambled from her seat.

Before she could get to the berth, the door to the main cabin burst open and three AK-47-armed men dressed all in black stormed inside. They wore dark bandannas over the lower halves of their faces and black beanie caps over their heads so all that was visible were their eyes. Cold, menacing eyes.

Kyle recognized the men for what they were—mercenaries. Here in Chicago. Whoever was after Brenda had cash and connections. He wondered why they hadn't come in with a spray of gunfire.

"Don't do anything stupid," one of the masked gunmen said, gesturing with an AK-47.

Kyle's finger twitched on his weapon's trigger, but obviously he was outgunned. With a growl, he lowered his weapon. There was no way he could take down all three men before one of them started firing.

And that wasn't an option. Brenda would most certainly be killed if he got twitchy, although he feared she may be dead before this night was over anyway. Guilt for failing to protect her burned like acid in his gut. How had they been found?

He lifted his chin and stepped in front of her. His body wouldn't be much of a shield against the firepower aimed at his heart, but it was all he had, and he'd protect her with his life.

Not because it was his job, but because his feelings ran deep. Deeper than he even wanted to admit.

Lifting his hands and hoping there was still a way out of this, Kyle said, "We don't want any trouble."

One of the masked gunmen stepped closer. "Trouble don't care. It's here."

Kyle held his ground. If the guy was dumb enough to come within striking distance, Kyle just might have a chance of turning this nightmare around. He took a half step closer. "What do you want?"

"We'll get what we want when the doctor's dead."

Brenda gasped.

"Why?" Kyle moved forward, his muscles firing, ready to attack.

The business end of the AK-47 raised level to Kyle's eyes. "Back off."

The guy wasn't so dumb after all. Kyle stepped backward. "You can either die now or with the doctor. Your choice."

Assessing his options, Kyle stalled. "She at least deserves to know who wants her dead."

"We're not paid to answer questions," the man barked out. "Now both of you, inside the bedroom cabin."

Okay, so they didn't intend to shoot them outright. Good. Excellent, actually. Maybe they had a shot at escaping. Kyle backed Brenda into the cabin. Once they were inside, the leader motioned for one of his goons to enter. The man secured their hands and feet with plastic zip ties before leaving, locking the door behind him.

"What are they going to do?" Fear, stark and vivid, flickered in her dark eyes.

His chest knotted.

She sat on the end of the bed as if her legs wouldn't hold her up any longer. He didn't blame her.

Kyle could come up with several scenarios. None of which ended well for them. He had to get them out of there fast. He sat next to Brenda and kicked off his shoes. With his bound hands, he managed to get his pant leg up to reveal his butterfly knife sheathed in a leather pouch strapped high on his calf.

Swinging his legs over Brenda's lap, he said, "Grab the knife."

She managed to slide the weapon from the sheath just as a loud explosion filled the air. The vessel shuddered. Brenda screamed. The boat keeled to the right. Unsecured, Kyle and Brenda went tumbling across the bed to land in a heap against the wall. The knife skittered across the blue carpet and clattered to a stop against the wood a few feet away.

Commando-crawling, Kyle reached the knife and worked the blade beneath the plastic tie binding his feet together.

Brenda lay motionless on the wall that now was their floor. Icy fear froze his blood. He quickly cut her bonds, realizing she'd hit her head when they'd crashed into the wall. A nasty red lump formed above her temple.

"Come on, Brenda, wake up," Kyle said, his voice thick with urgency.

He stuck the handle of the knife between his teeth and brought his hands up to cut the zip tie. Once his hands were free, he gathered Brenda into his arms. Water seeped in from the cracks around the door. The rushing sound of water filling the hull roared in Kyle's ears. The cabin door bowed under the pressure. Any second the hinges would give and the room would fill. Kyle wasn't afraid for himself. He could swim out no sweat. But with Brenda unconscious, he couldn't stop her from breathing in the lake water and drowning. He needed her awake.

Panic flared white-hot. He patted her cheeks. "Come on, honey, wake up."

She stirred and batted at his hands. "What? Stop."

Relieved, Kyle pressed his lips to her forehead. "Okay, time to get out of here."

"What happened?"

"You hit your head. I hope you can swim," he said.

"Of course I can swim." Her gaze shifted away from his. She gasped. "We've tipped over. We're taking on water."

"Yep on both accounts." He slid an arm around her waist. "Any second now that door is going to give, and this room will fill with water. I want you to be ready."

She swallowed. "Ready to die?"

Her tone hinged on the edge of hysteria. He needed her to stay calm. "No. You're not going to die. I won't let you."

"Why is this happening? Who wants me dead so badly?"

Kyle wished he had answers. But he was more concerned with getting to the surface. The door creaked. One hinge popped. "We've got to move."

He hustled her to the far corner, where they wouldn't be in the direct path of the water when it crashed through the door. "Deep breath. Fill your lungs."

She did.

"Again."

Just as they both sucked in air, the door gave. A crush

of cold water flooded the room, quickly filling the space and chasing away the air. Buoyant, Kyle treaded water and let the rising tide carry him and Brenda upward toward the portside window. As the water rose, covering their chins, he used the blade to dig out the edges of the glass in the porthole.

"Kyle?" Brenda had her nose and mouth pressed against the wood. Water lapped at her face, threatening to cover her completely.

"Hold tight." He worked the glass from the pane. He gulped in air. "Here. Breathe." He needed to find a way out of this watery coffin. "I'll be right back."

He pushed her toward the opening, which was just big enough for her to stick her face through. Sheathing his knife, he dived beneath the water to swim through the door into the main cabin and up to the surface, counting the seconds as he went. He broke free of the water and gasped for air. An easy two minutes underwater. The yacht was on its side and quickly going under. Moonlight reflected on the sailboat's hull, where a gaping hole had been ripped into the aft. Their assailants had used C-4. Not enough to blow them completely out of the water, just enough to sink the boat.

Kyle reached the window. Brenda's fingers gripping the edge and her pale face were the only things he could see.

"I'm coming in to get you. But I need you to listen carefully," he said.

She nodded. Light from the moon showed the dilation of her dark pupils. She was going into shock.

"When I come to you, I'll tap your shoulder. When I do that, you take a deep breath and hold it. Then you're going to put your arms around my neck and we'll swim out."

"I can't do that," she said.

"Yes, you can. I know you can."

"No. No," she said, her voice rising with hysteria.

"Yes. Listen to me. You can do this. We can do this."

She closed her eyes.

Afraid she was giving up, he shouted, "Look at me." Her lids popped open.

"I'll be right there. Hang on."

"Kyle!"

"Lord, we really need You now," he shouted as he made his way toward the opening that would lead him back to her. "Please. Please, let me get her out alive."

He inhaled and then dived under the water, sending up a constant litany of prayer to God that he made it to Brenda in time.

Brenda clung to the edges of the window. Her teeth chattered. Her limbs grew numb. She was tired of treading water. Wasn't even sure her feet were moving anymore. She couldn't feel anything. Hypothermia would set in soon. Despair threatened to devour her as she waited for Kyle to return. How could he be so confident they'd get out of this alive?

Because he had God on his side.

She'd heard his shouted prayer. Even in the face of certain disaster he cried out to God.

Feeling an urgency that welled from deep within, she drew on all the Sunday-school lessons her parents had dragged her to as a child and lifted up the only prayer her frantic mind could muster.

"Oh, God, please help us," she cried out, her voice barely more than a whisper. Hot tears welled and dripped into the lake water closing over her face.

She felt the tap on her shoulder. Relief mitigated with

terror spread through her. Her fingers flexed around the edges of the window, unwilling to give up the connection to the surface. But she had to. She couldn't let Kyle down by not trusting him now when it mattered the most. He was counting on her to follow him.

If she didn't let go, she'd die.

She wasn't ready to die. She wanted to live. Wanted to see where this relationship with Kyle could go. Wanted to tell him she was falling in love with him.

Determined to live, she inhaled deeply and filled her lungs to bursting and let go.

Kyle's hand pulled her beneath the surface of the water into what was supposed to have been their watery grave. She nearly panicked as the air in her chest threatened to expel. Kyle guided her arms around his neck. She clung to him, her chest pressing against the solid strength of his back. She closed her eyes tight and fought the urge to breathe. She felt almost as if she was flying as Kyle's powerful body cut through the water, pulling her along.

She banged her foot against the doorjamb of the main cabin, but her limbs were so cold, so numb, she'd barely registered any pain. Her eyes popped open to darkness. She could feel a scream building even though her sluggish brain told her they were in the stairwell that led to the deck. She held on to Kyle as he swam them up and up.

Her lungs burned. Her body felt heavy. Her mind screamed for oxygen.

She couldn't hold out much longer.

Then they cleared the surface. The cool night air hit her face. She dragged in a gulping breath of lifesaving oxygen. Kyle held on to her and swam away from the boat, keeping her upright in the choppy waves as the lake overcame the boat and pulled the craft beneath the surface of the water.

They hadn't gone down with the ship. But they were three miles offshore in freezing water with no life preservers. Their chances of survival were slim.

What could be worse?

Then she felt the drops of rain as the dark clouds she'd seen earlier on the horizon let loose.

Hysteria bubbled. A disbelieving laugh escaped. "Won—dder—fful," she said between clattering teeth.

"That's the spirit," Kyle said, his white teeth flashing in the muted moonlight.

"How can you be grinning?" she snapped.

He spun her around and pointed toward the smattering of lights dotting the shore. "Three miles. No sweat."

"Maybe for you," she muttered. The only thing keeping her from sinking was his arm around her waist.

"I'll be right here with you," he said.

"I'm so cold," she said, fearing her arms and legs wouldn't work.

"You'll warm up once you start moving."

Dredging up what little strength remained in her body, she started to slowly move, kicking her legs and pulling her arms through the waves in a breaststroke style. Water splashed in her face. Got into her mouth, the taste setting off her gag reflex. She spit the nasty water out and pressed her lips tight. Kyle kept his hand on her hip as he sideswam next to her. She focused on the dots along the shore.

But it was rugged going and before long exhaustion slowed her movements. She struggled to continue. She was so tired. She wanted to sleep.

"Brenda!"

Kyle's voice jolted her. She sputtered, dipping beneath the surface. Strong hands grasped her and lifted her head above the waterline. She felt her world turn on its axis as he flipped her onto her back. She stared upward at the dark sky overhead. Rain pelted her face. Arms slid beneath her armpits. Then she was gliding through the water. Her mind fought to understand what he was doing, how they were going to survive, but she was so cold. So tired. Her eyelids shut. The rush of water in her ears slowly faded into nothingness, and her last thought was that she'd lost Kyle before she'd even really had him.

ELEVEN

Kyle's feet found purchase on the shore. He'd long since kicked off his shoes. His toes dug into the sand. Relief rivaling what he'd experienced after surviving Hell Week during BUD/S training at Coronado washed over him as he dragged Brenda out of the water.

During his training, he and his fellow recruits had been pushed to the limit of physical fortitude and mental determination. Two-thirds of the men who'd started the training had called it quits by ringing the bell. To this day, Kyle shuddered at the sound. He'd wanted to ring that bell so badly, but he'd been too stubborn, refusing to give up, to break, and had gutted it out.

His biceps strained from having been flexed for so long as he lifted Brenda's unconscious body into his arms and started walking. His soaking-wet cargo pants added weight to his fatigued legs. The beach gave way to trees, the trees to a dark road. Up ahead the glow of a gas station beckoned.

No cars sat at the pumps. Kyle pushed open the door to the minimart. Little chimes sounded overhead. The guy behind the counter stared as Kyle trudged inside, water dripping off him and Brenda to puddle on the floor.

"Call 911." Kyle barked out the command then slowly sank to his knees and gently eased Brenda onto the dry floor. Warmth from the store seeped into his muscles and bones, firing off his nerve endings with little jolts of electricity. His numb fingers tingled, burned. He checked her pulse. Glad to feel the steady beat, he sat back against the counter and held her close, his heart filling with a tenderness so strong he feared he might finally break.

He'd come close to losing her tonight. She'd become more to him than a client he was protecting. She'd become the woman who'd captured his heart. And he would never be the same.

How was he going to leave her when the time came?

Brenda awoke to find herself in a hospital bed. Monitors beeped. An IV dripped.

Where was Kyle?

Somehow, someway, he'd kept her safe and alive. She had to see him. Wanted to make sure he was okay, as well.

She tried to move. Pain exploded everywhere.

Staring at the generic white ceiling found in most hospital facilities, she tried to assess the damage to her body. Her fatigued muscles and sore limbs needed time to heal. Her head pounded. Her ankle throbbed.

The last thing she remembered was treading water in the cold lake after masked gunmen had sunk her father's boat. And had meant for her to die, trapped inside a watery grave. Her stomach heaved with the horrible thought.

If not for Kyle, she'd be dead. He was an amazing man, honorable and brave. A man she was rapidly falling for.

A rumbly, out-of-place noise sent her heart pounding. She jerked toward the sound. Her neck muscles zinged and pain hammered against her temples at the movement.

But the sight of Kyle sitting in a chair, his chin resting on his chest, brought a sigh of relief. He was safe. A rush of affection flowed over her as she watched him.

He'd changed into a dry, dark long-sleeve shirt and jeans. She took a moment to watch him sleep as tender emotions flooded through her system. His dark eyelashes kissed his cheeks. His tousled hair gave him a boyish air. But she knew better.

He was a man of action. A man who'd risked his life for her, had protected her and somehow delivered her to safety when she'd given up any hope of surviving.

Thankful to be alive, her soul rejoiced. God had answered her prayers. A peace she'd never known wove through her. Though faith defied logic, she chose to believe in God.

She wasn't sure exactly what to do with that belief, but she knew someone she could ask. Kyle.

"It's rude to stare," he murmured, his lips barely moving.

She blinked as heat traveled up her neck and stung her cheeks. Not asleep after all. Why was she surprised? The man was never what he seemed. He was so much more than she'd imagined. And she liked that. Liked him. "I thought maybe I was dreaming. We made it."

"We did."

"How did we get here?"

He opened one eye. "By ambulance."

Not what she'd meant. "Did you tow me all the way to shore?"

Lifting his head, he stretched. "Yep."

She'd come to realize he'd do anything to protect her. "How did you call for help?"

"There was a gas station a mile down the road."

She wasn't fooled by his nonchalant tone. "You carried me to the gas station?"

He shrugged. "You don't weigh much."

Affection wrapped around her. She held out her hand. "Thank you."

He folded his hand over hers, the pressure warm and secure. "You're welcome."

His blue eyes held her enthralled. Her heart sped up. The feelings crowding her chest were sliding beyond affection into uncharted territory. She needed to study these emotions, dissect them before she made any rash conclusions or declarations. "Where are we?"

"Rush University Medical Center. They were closest."

"Do I have hypothermia?"

"Yes. And a concussion. You were unconscious when they admitted you."

She frowned. "How long have we been here?"

"Since early yesterday morning."

Surprise rocked her. She'd been unconscious for at least twenty-four hours. "What time is it?"

"After nine. Good morning." He grinned. "You were exhausted."

Not nearly as much as she'd guess he was. "Have you slept?"

"I just was," he said.

"A catnap at best," she stated. "You rescue-swam with me from the middle of the lake. Carried me a mile. You can't tell me you weren't exhausted, too."

"I won't tell you that. It would be a lie. I was exhausted, though it wasn't the middle of the lake. Three miles offshore max." His smile turned tender. "I did sleep last night. And your concern is touching."

His intense gaze made little butterflies dance inside her tummy. She tried to sit up. Every muscle protested. Kyle shot to his feet to offer his assistance.

Once upright, she asked, "Did they find the men who tried to kill us?"

Kyle ran a hand through his hair, creating even more havoc with his blond mane. "No. The police are in the process of dredging up your dad's boat. But there won't be anything to lead us to the man who wants you dead."

"You sound so sure."

"I am. Those men were professional mercenaries."

"How can you be sure they weren't just hired thugs off the street?"

"It was in their eyes and the way they held their weapons. Those were military-trained men. Mercs willing to hire out to the highest bidder. There's no loyalty or honor involved. It's just about the money."

Clearly he had little tolerance for the type of man who would use his skills for illegal gain. Who could hate her so much that they'd pay to have her killed? What had she done to deserve this?

As if he'd read her thoughts, he said, "We'll figure it out."

How did he do that? He offered comfort and assurance without being prompted. He was so in tune to her. It left her feeling unbalanced, unsettled and...known. She couldn't remember anyone ever making her feel so cared for, so special. And that scared and thrilled her at the same time, because she wanted more. Wanted to be more than the person he was protecting.

He smoothed back her hair. "Right now you need

to concentrate on gaining back your strength. Are you hungry?"

For a kiss. No, not now. But soon, she hoped. "I could eat. Maybe some eggs, toast. Nothing too heavy."

He hit the nurse's call button. A few minutes later a tall, pretty red-haired woman arrived. She wore a multicolored smock over lightweight scrubs.

"I'm glad to see our patient has awoken. I'm Nurse Nancy," she said with a wide smile. "I'll let Dr. Reece know."

"She'd like to order breakfast, as well," Kyle said.

"I'll take your breakfast order after I get the doctor," the nurse said.

As soon as she disappeared out the door, Kyle asked, "Do you know Dr. Reece?"

"No. I'm not familiar with this facility."

The door to the room opened and a short man of about fifty walked in. He had graying hair and kind eyes. "Dr. Storm, so glad to see you awake. I'm Dr. Reece." He held out his hand. His handshake was firm. Her fingers stung. "I was on call yesterday when you were brought in. How are you feeling?"

"Stiff. A little headachy."

He nodded. "You had a mild concussion and hypothermia."

She vaguely remembered hitting her head. No wonder it hurt as if she'd taken a hit from a loose boom. She'd done that once when she'd first learned how to sail. She hadn't been paying attention, too excited by the freedom of the water. The boom had worked itself loose and struck her alongside the head. The blow hadn't been enough to knock her out, but enough to give her a horrible headache for a few days.

"The stiffness will wear off once you're up and moving," Dr. Reece continued. "I can give you meds to help with the headache. I'd caution not to overexert yourself for the next day or so. Drink plenty of fluids, and rest."

All advice she'd given a hundred times before. It felt odd to be on this side of the bed. She wasn't used to being taken care of.

"Thank you, Doctor," she said, liking him and his bedside manner and realizing she needed to work on her own. "How soon can I be released?"

"I'll put the order in now. Nancy tells me you have an appetite. By the time you've had breakfast you should be ready to go."

"Actually, I'd just as soon eat elsewhere," Brenda stated. She'd had her fill of eating from the hospital kitchen during her years as a med student, intern and resident.

"By all means," Dr. Reece said with a smile. "I'll get the ball rolling on your release."

When he left, Kyle held up a department-store bag. "I had fresh clothes delivered from the store for you."

"You think of everything. Thank you," Brenda said, liking how thoughtful he was.

Kyle stood to leave to give her privacy. As soon as the door shut behind him, she opened the bag and pulled out the clothes. He'd thought of everything. The vibrant red blouse and stylish jeans were not something she would have picked for herself, but she'd already learned he liked bright and flashy.

Something she wasn't.

Her chest tightened. He had wormed his way into her heart, her life. But no matter how she dressed, she'd never be the type of woman he'd want.

Disappointment seized her.

She'd be deluding herself if she tried to pretend she

was, no matter how much she wished she could be. Okay, they enjoyed each other's company. He was considerate and kind, had saved her life numerous times, but that didn't mean he cared beyond what was required. Who was she kidding? She was a job to him.

She'd better tuck her feelings away and protect herself, or she'd end up brokenhearted. But she had a feeling keeping herself immune to him would be the hardest thing she'd ever had to face when he kept proving himself to be a good man, a man she wanted to love.

Kyle stood down the hall, talking to Detective Lebowitz. He angled himself so he could keep an eye on Brenda's room. Not that she wasn't fully protected with an armed police officer sitting outside the door, which Lebowitz had arranged so Kyle could get a few hours of rest.

The detective had stopped by to give an update on the progress of the case. He'd reinterviewed the family involved with the lawsuit against Brenda and the hospital and still came up empty.

Kyle wasn't surprised. This threat on Brenda's life seemed too personal to be an issue involving the hospital, too. This felt almost like a vendetta.

Brenda's door opened and she stepped out. Beautiful! He'd known the red top would complement her with her dark hair and creamy complexion. And the jeans molded to her curves in all the right places. The trendy athletic shoes made her feet look small and dainty.

She hesitated in the doorway; her big brown eyes looked so vulnerable until her gaze locked on him like a guidance missile. Then her nerves seemed to settle. A soft smile touched her lips. A smile meant only for him. An explosion of emotion ripped through him, leaving him feeling as if he'd air-dropped a twenty-foot wave. Thrilling and terrifying at the same time.

A chirping sounded from his pocket. Using the interruption as an excuse to catch his breath, Kyle broke eye contact with Brenda to dig a new smartphone out of one of his pants pockets and checked the screen. "Our ride is here."

Brenda looked at the phone with curiosity. "When did you get that?"

"Trent had it sent over." He'd also assigned reinforcements who were waiting downstairs. Kyle had asked for the help. This assignment had turned out to be more complicated than any of them had expected. With a team in place, Brenda would be that much safer. And that was all that mattered.

"I need to replace my pager," she said.

He stilled. "Pager?"

"It's at the bottom of Lake Michigan."

"You always carry one?"

"Yes, I'm rarely without it."

"You had one with you on the yacht?"

She tilted her head. "I did." Her eyes widened. "Do you think that's how those men found us?"

"Pagers don't transmit a signal, but only act as a receiver, so no, I wouldn't say that is how they found us…unless someone placed a transmitter in the device." Which seemed likely. Given someone had access to the hospital and her operating room, they could have easily snuck a transmitter into her pager at a time when she didn't have it in her possession.

Lebowitz stepped forward. "Dr. Storm. I want to assure you we are doing everything in our power to find out who's after you."

Brenda inclined her head to the detective. "I'm sure you are, Detective. Thank you."

"Can I get your new number?" Lebowitz asked Kyle.

Being extra cautious, Kyle said, "If you need to reach me, contact Trent Associates."

Lebowitz's lips thinned. "Very well. If you need anything, don't hesitate. Chicago P.D. wants to be of service."

They said goodbye to the detective and Dr. Reece. When they exited the hospital, Kyle stopped short.

A bright yellow monster of an SUV sat idling at the curb.

Leave it to Trevor to pick the most conspicuous vehicle he could find.

"Is that our ride?" Brenda asked, staring at the beast as if it might rear on its hind legs and charge at them.

With a wry grin, he said, "Yep. Afraid so."

The driver's-side door opened. Trevor Jordon climbed out with a huge smile on his face. Big, tall and bald, the ex-paratrooper was as brash as they came. Which in most cases served Trent Associates well. Today, however, Kyle would have preferred a bit more discretion.

"What, you couldn't find the most outrageous vehicle possible?" Kyle said as he clapped his friend and fellow bodyguard's hand and squeezed.

Trevor gave as good as he got. "It was this or a Prius. I can't fit in a Prius."

"Yeah, me neither." Kyle slid a hand to the back of Brenda's lower back. "Meet Dr. Storm." He caught the slight hitch to Trevor's brows. Appreciation and interest flared in the younger man's eyes. Kyle cleared his throat. "Our client," he said pointedly.

"Ma'am," Trevor said.

"Brenda, meet Trevor Jordon."

"Hello." She turned to give Kyle a quizzical look.

Before he could explain, the back passenger door opened. A wild head of blond curls and an impish face appeared over the top of the door. "Enough chewing the fat, people. We're drawing enough attention as it is in this monstrosity without advertising where the doctor is."

The woman shook her head, her piercing blue gaze landing on Brenda. "I'm just going to apologize now for these two lugheads." She waved toward the car. "Come on and climb in here, Doc." Then she disappeared back inside the belly of the vehicle.

"That's Jackie Blain," Kyle said with a wry grin. "She's a firecracker."

"I'll second that," Trevor commented. "We've got a safe house all set up." He climbed into the driver's seat. "Let's roll."

"What are they doing here?" Brenda asked, following him into the yellow vehicle.

"I asked for them."

She paused and put a hand on Kyle's arm. "Thank you."

He cocked his head to the side. "For?"

"For everything. For them." Though she couldn't help the ribbon of disappointment that it would not be just them anymore.

His grin hit her in the solar plexus. "I'm not a martyr. The guy trying to kill you has got a team. Now we've got a team. It's almost fair."

Brenda swallowed back the spurt of fear as his words brought back their earlier conversation. The man who wanted her dead had hired mercenaries. Men who would kill her without remorse. She shuddered. "Almost?"

He winked. "They're gonna get whipped."

* * *

The safe house was an older brick, single-family townhome in the neighborhood known as Uptown, just six miles north of The Loop, Chicago's historic commercial center.

Brenda was surprised by the interior of the house. Gleaming cherry hardwood floors, leather-upholstered furniture and dark wood cabinets gave the place an updated feel.

Trevor carried in two duffel bags and set them on the dining-room table. "We brought toys."

She didn't think they were talking board games or cards. Raising an eyebrow, Brenda looked to Kyle for explanation.

He unzipped a bag and held up a gun that even to her untrained eye was high caliber.

She supposed in their world guns were toys. And the ones with the biggest and the baddest ones won.

She hated this. Hated what this person had thrust her into by wanting her dead.

"Isn't this great," Jackie exclaimed as she plopped down on the leather sofa, yanked off her short black boots and tucked her bright-sock-clad feet beneath her. "Come on, Doc, take a load off while the boys wait on us."

"Who owns this place?" Brenda asked, sitting down on the couch.

Jackie shrugged. "Don't know. James, that's our boss, made the arrangements. I wouldn't doubt it if he'd bought the property."

"Trent Associates must do well, then," Brenda commented, thinking the townhome would go for close to a million on the open market. She wondered what the hospital was paying for three bodyguards. Whatever the price, she was thankful.

Kyle gave her a grin. "Told you. We're good."

He was good. Her heart flipped in her chest. When he left the room, she missed him.

"So, Kyle's filled us in," Jackie stated, her crystal-blue eyes assessing. She pulled out a notepad and pen from her leather satchel she'd brought inside the town-home with her. "But I'd like to hear the details from you." She wrinkled her upturned nose. "You know men, just the facts."

They shared a smile, and Brenda decided she liked the petite blonde. She'd never had many close friends growing up, always too busy studying to really form any tight bonds. Settling back, Brenda started at the beginning with the delivery of the cupcakes and finished with waking up in the hospital this morning.

Jackie listened, her intelligent eyes never wavering as she furiously wrote on her notepad. "Interesting," she finally said after Brenda fell silent.

Trevor appeared in the doorway. "Hey, ladies, brunch is served."

Jackie was on her feet and headed toward the dining room before Brenda had even straightened.

Kyle leaned against the archway. "You coming?"

She sat back against the buttery-leather cushion, wishing he'd sit down with her, hold her close and tell her everything would be okay.

"Hey." He pushed away from the wall. "You're safe now."

"I wish this was over."

He sat across from her on the coffee table. Their knees touched. She took comfort in the slight contact.

"It will be soon," he said.

And then she could resume her life. Go back to her career, back to Sunday dinners with her parents. A wave of homesickness hit her. "I'd like to check on my father."

He nodded. "We can arrange a phone call. Trevor bought several burner phones. Also, I called Dr. Landsem to let him know you were safe. He said you're scheduled for a deposition tomorrow in the Hanson case. Apparently the hospital's attorney is freaking out because he needs to speak to you."

A knot formed in her chest. "In the chaos of the last few days the lawsuit slipped my mind."

"We'll get through this."

The promise in his voice unfurled a ribbon of relief through her. She wasn't exactly sure when, but somewhere along the way she'd come to rely on Kyle not only for her safety, but her peace of mind.

"How long will you be here?" She blurted the question without filtering. She held her breath, almost afraid to hope he'd say forever and realizing how desperately she wanted him to.

He took her hand, his strong fingers curving over hers like a protective cover.

"As long as it takes," he said. "I'm not leaving you until this is over."

Disappointment dropped like a stone in her tummy. "Until your assignment is over, you mean."

His eyebrows dipped. "Brenda—"

She held up a hand. "Of course you'll leave then. I'll be out of danger and won't need you."

A flash of something close to hurt or maybe regret crossed his face. "That's how it works. I come, do my job and then I leave. And all of this will be a memory."

A memory that would bring pain and fear and sorrow, because against her will he'd managed to breach the barricades she'd erected around her heart.

And she didn't know how or if she'd be able to re-build the protective barrier in time to keep herself from being totally heartbroken when he left.

TWELVE

"Jackie was a deputy sheriff for a small town in the Midwest," Kyle explained later that afternoon as they drove across town toward Heritage Hospital. He knew Brenda well enough to know she needed all the facts to feel comfortable. "She thinks if we go through your files, we'll find clues that will lead us to the killer."

"Maybe, but there's this little issue called doctor-patient confidentiality," Brenda said. She sat in the backseat next to Jackie.

"*We* don't have to lay eyes on the files, but we need you to," Jackie stated. She sat behind Trevor with the window halfway down. Her blond curls whipped around her head, making her appear younger than twenty-nine.

"What will I be looking for?"

"That's the million-dollar question," Jackie said cryptically.

Kyle could see the anxiety in Brenda's expression and knew the flip answer wouldn't suffice. Brenda liked things straightforward. "As you go through the files, look for anything out of the ordinary, anything that could give any of your patients reason to want to get revenge on you."

"Revenge," Brenda said softly. "I hadn't thought of

it that way." She nodded as determination firmed her jaw. "Okay. I'll gather everything from my office. Do you think we should collect my files from the clinic, as well?"

Kyle smiled with approval. "Yes, I do."

She held his gaze for a moment. He saw the trust and confidence in her dark eyes. Something intense passed between them. If they'd been alone he would have drawn her into his embrace. But they weren't alone, and the back of the seat separated them. Which was a good thing because he was getting too involved with his client. And he had a feeling she was becoming attached, as well. It wasn't unusual for a protectee to develop feelings for the one protecting him or her. She was placing her life in his hands. Going one step further and placing her heart there, too, wasn't a huge leap. But he knew better. He knew the intensity of the situation had a way of clouding one's thoughts. It was certainly clouding his, because all he could think about was Brenda.

With effort he shifted toward the road ahead. His gaze caught the amused glint in Jackie's perceptive eyes.

Could she see what was happening between him and Brenda?

Heat crept up the back of his neck. Kyle needed to do a better job of hiding his attraction and affection for his client. Becoming emotionally involved with a protectee tended to impair a bodyguard's judgment.

At least Kyle told himself as much. He chose to ignore the living contradiction that was his buddy and fellow Trent associate Don Cavanaugh. Don had taken on a client last Christmas only to fall head over heels in love during the course of the assignment. The two had recently married, in fact. Not a path Kyle had any intention of traveling down. He wasn't a commitment type of guy.

Or at least he'd never wanted to commit to one woman until a certain dark-eyed doctor wove her way into his heart. Now he could envision staying in Chicago, spending his days and nights with Brenda. Could imagine weekends out on the lake, teaching her how to windsurf, her teaching him how to sail.

Giving himself a mental shake, he told himself to keep it together. Stay focused on the assignment, not his growing feelings for his client.

At Heritage Hospital they took her computer and boxed up her files without incident. Then they headed downtown. Kyle was impressed with the clinic Brenda had helped establish. Though the outside of the nondescript, flat-roofed, yellow-brick building wasn't attractive, the inside was anything but drab. Bold-colored walls, bright, comfortable furniture and friendly smiles from the staff and faculty gave the free clinic a welcoming air.

The place hummed with activity. Several patients called out greetings to Brenda as she led the way to the back offices. She flipped on the light in the space and froze. File cabinets were open and folders haphazardly stuck out. Her computer had been smashed. Bits and pieces of plastic and glass were all over the desk and floor.

"Okay, everyone step back," Jackie said, pushing her way in the office. "The place needs to be dusted before we remove the files." She took a pair of latex gloves from her satchel and slipped them over her small hands. She inspected the computer. "Not sure anything will be recoverable off here."

"I back everything up on a thumb drive," Brenda said.

"Where do you keep it?" Kyle asked.

"In my locker in the changing room," she said.

Taking her by the elbow, Kyle said, "Show me."

She took him to the women's employee locker room and stopped before a full-length locker secured with a combination lock. The place where a name should be was blank. Brenda quickly spun the dial and unlocked the locker. She opened the door. A pair of shoes sat on the top shelf. A white lab coat hung on a hook.

She reached into the pocket of the coat and brought out a small, flowered thumb drive and held it up triumphantly. "Ta-da."

Affection swelled in his chest. He closed his hand over hers. "Awesome. You're awesome."

His gaze dropped to her perfectly bowed mouth then lifted back to her eyes. The longing in the dark depths made him suck in a charged breath. It would be so easy to dip his head, to capture her lips, to give over to the anticipation building in his blood.

Her lips parted.

An invitation?

He shifted closer, hovering, waiting. He'd never take without permission.

To his intense joy, she rose to meet him. Their lips touched. Her mouth molded sweetly to his, jolting his senses as if short-circuited. He slipped a hand behind her head, drawing closer, increasing the pressure. Her arms wound around his neck. Pleasure radiated outward from where their mouths joined. He lost himself in the moment.

"Hey," Trevor called from the doorway. "Police are here."

Jerked to reality, Kyle broke the kiss.

Brenda's dazed expression mirrored the bemusement bouncing around his head and his heart.

She stepped back, touched a shaky hand to her lips before spinning away and practically running for the door of the locker room. She pushed past Trevor and disappeared out of sight. Trevor raised a questioning eyebrow at Kyle before following their client.

Rocked on his heels, Kyle needed a moment to regroup.

He'd kissed the doctor until his senses had ignited, threatening to incinerate them both. And she'd kissed him back with a fierceness that had not only surprised him, but by her reaction had caught her off guard, as well. Her control had slipped, revealing the warm and passionate woman he'd seen glimpses of beneath the reserved exterior. A woman he was rapidly falling for.

Raking a hand through his hair, he wondered when he'd lost his mind. He had no business toying with the doctor's affections. He would be leaving when the threat to her life had been neutralized. Confusing the situation by allowing their association to become personal was a mistake. A mistake that could cost, or cause, them both heartache.

Forget any more kisses. And no more contemplation about a future together. That wasn't possible. He wasn't staying in Chicago, and he'd never ask her to leave with him.

Determined to keep himself in check and their relationship strictly professional, he went to find his client and do his job.

Jackie set the two boxes full of files on the kitchen table of the townhome. "This should keep you busy."

Brenda attacked the files with gusto, glad to have

something to concentrate on, something to distract her from the disturbing and oh-so-wonderful memory of Kyle's kiss.

Using every ounce of single-minded concentration that had served her well all through med school, she examined each file, trying to recall the patient and any reason he or she would have to want revenge on her.

But her careful, clinically detailed notes held no personal musings, no indicators that she'd taken any notice of the patients beyond the illnesses that had brought them to her for care.

How could she have performed so many surgeries, yet have no personal connection to any of these patients? The question pounded at her as she worked her way through one box, then another.

And even more disturbing was the question of why was she now realizing how much she wanted connections?

Kyle.

That was why. He'd crashed into her world and stirred up longings that had lain dormant her whole life.

She wanted to be connected. She wanted to form bonds and ties. She wanted to be loved and to love. The romantic girl who'd once naively given her heart to the wrong man now wanted a chance to try again.

But did she have the courage?

Around midnight, Kyle put his hand on her shoulder, sending tendrils of pleasure sliding through her. The memory of his kiss charged to the front of her mind, making her heart speed up. Making her want a repeat performance, if for no other reason than for those few short moments, she'd not been afraid or alone, but had felt safe and connected to Kyle.

Had he felt the same? Did it matter?

"That's enough for tonight," he said. "Give it a rest."

Frustration blasted through Brenda on so many levels. "If the answer's somewhere in these stacks of files, I'm not seeing it."

"You may discover something in the computer files." He held out his hand. "But right now you need to rest. You have a big day tomorrow. Or rather, today."

The deposition. Anxiety knotted in her chest. She allowed Kyle to lead her to her room, her hand encased within his warm grip.

"I'm right across the hall," he said, releasing her hand and stepping back.

"Kyle."

He raised an eyebrow. "Yes?"

She wanted to ask him about the kiss. Had it meant anything to him? Did she mean anything to him?

The words stuck in her throat. What if he said no, the kiss hadn't meant anything to him? She meant nothing to him? Her courage failed her. Better not to ask than risk being hurt.

"Good night," she managed before escaping into her room.

She tried to sleep, but dreams and nightmares tormented her mind until she finally gave up and returned to the kitchen just before 6:00 a.m. to continue her perusal of the files.

When she walked in, Kyle was already sitting at the table doing his devotions. He stood and went to the counter, where a pot of coffee steamed. He poured a mug and set it on the table beside her. "I'm making French toast for breakfast."

She leaned her chin on her hand and gazed up at him with yearnings stirring in her heart. She could imagine more mornings like this with him. She could imagine coming home at the end of the day to a home they shared. Against her better judgment, she imagined spending the rest of her life with him. "You're spoiling me."

He flashed a grin. Her breath caught and held.

"You'll need your energy for today," he said.

Reality intruded on her dreamy state of mind. The deposition. She straightened, focusing her mind on the day rather than her attraction to her bodyguard. "Yes, I will."

She wouldn't exactly appear competent dressed in jeans and tennis shoes. "I'll need to go to my apartment for something more appropriate to wear."

"Make a list of what you need. I'll send Jackie and Trevor to retrieve it."

Though he didn't say it, she understood his words implied that it wasn't safe yet to go back to her apartment. She wondered when or if it would ever be.

"I'll need to call Mason," she said. "I'm sure he's having a fit by now." The hospital's lawyer, Mason Debuois, was a bulldog of a man. Brenda didn't exactly feel comfortable with the man. He was too high-strung for her taste.

"Already taken care of," Kyle said. "Mr. Debuois will meet us thirty minutes early to prepare you."

He made things easier for her. Warmth floated through her veins. A smile spread across her face. In spite of the day facing her, Kyle grounded her, calmed her when all her insides wanted to quiver. "Thank you."

He saluted. "All part of the service."

Her smile faltered. "Right."

He wasn't trying to make things easier for her. Of course he'd take charge of setting up the meeting; he was paid to take care of details that related to her safety. That was his job.

Disappointment robbed her of the good feelings she'd been experiencing.

But deep inside, in places she didn't want to look at too closely, lurked a wish that she could be more than just a job to him.

A wish best kept hidden, even from herself.

Determined to stay on task and find some reason why someone wanted her dead, she squared her shoulders and dived back into the files.

Two hours later, stiff and tired, she asked Kyle if they could check on her father.

He handed her one of the burner phones.

She called the hospital but was told he'd been released. She dialed her parents' home number.

When her dad answered sounding more like himself, her heart squeezed tight with love. He was home and resting. The antibiotics had kicked the pneumonia. He felt better.

"Just make sure you rest and stay hydrated. Don't overdo it," she cautioned. "I love you. Tell Mom I love her, too."

She clicked off and handed Kyle back the phone. "He's home. When can I go see them?"

"Soon, I promise," Kyle answered with compassion in his blue eyes.

Brenda wanted to believe him. Needed to believe him. She knew he'd do all he could to make sure she could see her family.

The front door opened. Jackie and Trevor returning from Brenda's apartment.

"Here you go," Jackie said, handing over a garment bag. "Clothes for the deposition."

Taking the garment bag, Brenda went upstairs to change into the classic and stylish two-piece, dove-gray skirt suit from Danny & Nicole. The lovely four-button jacket with a bead-embellished shawl collar fit snuggly over a cream shell, and the knee-length matching skirt finished the look. She'd worn the outfit only once before, to a luncheon where she'd been given an award for outstanding community service. The expensive suit had been an impulse buy she normally didn't give in to. She usually chose her clothing for function rather than fashion.

When she came downstairs, Kyle let out a low whistle. Suddenly she was glad she'd splurged on the suit. She never cared what men thought about her style of dress, but Kyle's appreciation sent shivers of yearning skating over her. She felt feminine and pretty. A way she normally didn't feel wearing a white lab coat and a stethoscope for an accessory.

They arrived at the courthouse on time. Kyle walked beside Brenda while Trevor and Jackie broke off to blend in with the scenery.

"What are they doing?" Brenda asked.

"Keeping a watchful eye for anyone or anything questionable or threatening," Kyle replied in hushed tones. "They have our backs."

"That's good to know," she said, praying that nothing would happen. She just wanted this over with.

They found Mason waiting in an alcove on the second floor. He wore a brown tailored suit, white dress shirt and a paisley tie. His dark cropped hair was gelled back, making him look more like mafia than a lawyer.

"First, he can't come with you," Mason said as soon as she'd made the introductions.

"What?" She wanted Kyle to be in the room. She needed his strength, his calm.

"Not allowed."

Kyle took her hand and gave it a gentle squeeze. "I'll be right outside the door."

"Okay," Mason said sharply while pacing a short path in the alcove. His hand chopped the air. "So when we get in there, just tell a clear and believable account of Mr. Hanson's prep and surgery. Do not say anything that isn't a direct answer to a question. And under no circumstance are you to talk to the plaintiffs or their lawyer without me present."

As Mason continued his points on what to expect and how to act, Brenda nodded and strove for outward calm. But inside she was a mess. Nerves hit her stomach. Her palms felt sweaty. She couldn't remember the last time she'd been this nervous.

Panicked? Afraid? Terrified? Sure, too numerous to count over the past few days.

But this was different. Her career was at stake. Her reputation.

She tried to tell herself both were paltry issues compared with staying alive. Didn't help.

A uniformed officer stepped out of a room. "Hanson case."

Mason checked his watch. "Showtime."

Brenda sought Kyle's gaze. He gave her the thumbs-up sign. Knowing he'd be close gave her the courage to face the proceedings.

The deposition didn't take as long as she'd anticipated, nor was it as painful as she'd expected. She left the small, windowless room with her lawyer in tow. Kyle stood beside the door and fell into step beside her.

Halfway down the hall, Brenda came face-to-face

with Mr. Hanson's family. His widow, an elegantly dressed woman in her late sixties, stared at Brenda with glacial eyes full of hurt and sorrow.

Knowing the pain of her father's illness and how devastating it would be if he were to die without having an opportunity to say goodbye made Brenda's heart twist with empathy.

Sometimes people just need to know others understand. Kyle's words rang clearly inside her head. She'd come to understand what Kyle was trying to say that day. Brenda knew what she had to do. "Mrs. Hanson, may I speak with you?"

Behind her Mason sputtered, "Brenda, I advise against this."

One of the Hanson adult sons stepped in front of his mother. "We've been told not to speak to you."

Mrs. Hanson put a hand on her son's shoulder. "It's all right, dear. Let her have her say."

Brenda glanced at Kyle, saw his slight nod and knew she was doing the right thing. Ignoring Mason's protest, Brenda spoke with heartfelt honesty. "I did everything I could for your husband. I have gone over every detail of your husband's case, and I don't understand why he died."

Tears welled in Mrs. Hanson's eyes. Brenda felt them in her own eyes, as well.

"I'm heartsick over it and I apologize for whatever role I played in his death. I really did do everything in my power to save him."

One of the sons scoffed.

Mrs. Hanson held out her hand. Brenda took it.

"Thank you," Mrs. Hanson said. Then she turned and led her family into the deposition room.

As soon as they were alone, Mason threw up his hands. "You just lost the case."

Kyle slipped his arm around her waist. "I'm proud of you."

Basking in the glow of his words, she leaned into him, not caring whether it was a wise decision or not. She needed him, needed his strength, his calm, his support. "Thank—"

A piercing scream stopped her cold. Kyle's arm tightened around her, pulling her behind him as people ran for the exits.

Kyle's heart hammered in his chest. He touched his earpiece with his free hand. "Trevor, what's happening?"

Static crackled in his ear. The coms had gone out.

Uniformed officers urged everyone out of the building.

Keeping Brenda close, Kyle led her down the stairs. On the first-floor landing, he spotted Trevor. He jostled his way to their side.

"Hey, there's been some sort of bomb threat," Trevor explained. "Chicago P.D.'s got a bomb squad coming."

"The coms are being jammed," Kyle said, taking out the useless earpiece and putting it into his pocket.

"That was my thought, too. Police aren't doing it," Trevor said. "Jackie's bringing the vehicle around front."

If the circumstances weren't so tense, Kyle might have found the thought of Jackie driving the big yellow beast comical. But there was nothing funny about this situation. A random bomb threat wasn't a coincidence. Their adversary set this up. Kyle glanced at the courthouse door. Was a sniper waiting for Brenda to step outside?

Kyle looked for another way out. His gaze landed on a window facing the side street. "Tell Jackie to meet us on the south side of the building." Taking Brenda's hand, he tugged her forward as Trevor ran out the front door.

The window slid open wide enough for them to slip through. Even though they were technically on the first floor, there was a three-foot drop to the flower bed below the window. "I'll go first. As soon as I'm on the ground, I want you climbing out."

Brenda nodded.

Kyle climbed through and dropped easily to the ground. Brenda shimmied out the window. He placed his hands on her hips to help her to the ground.

The yellow SUV pulled to the curb. An expanse of lawn separated them from the safety of the vehicle.

"Keep low," Kyle cautioned. "We're going to run to the vehicle."

Brenda placed a hand on his shoulder to balance herself as she took off her shoes. Holding the shoes in one hand, she grasped his hand and said, "I'm ready."

In a low crouch they ran across the grass. The loud crack of a rifle jolted through Kyle. A bullet hit the ground inches from their feet as they hustled to the waiting vehicle. Brenda let out a terrified yelp. They dived inside the back passenger bay. Another bullet pinged off the vehicle's bumper.

Jackie gunned the engine and they shot away from the curb. She drove evasively for thirty minutes, taking side streets, random turns, double-backing and parking for a moment only to pull away from the curb after a couple of seconds. By the time they arrived at the safe house, Brenda was feeling not only frightened but also nauseous.

Once they were safely inside, she headed straight for her room at the far end of the second story. The whole ordeal had been exhausting. She took a face-plant on the bed and just lay there. Meeting with the lawyers, facing Mrs. Hanson and apologizing to running for her life, again, had taken a toll.

She didn't know how much more of this she could take. She felt like a mouse caught in a maze. Every move was blocked, every exit cut off, and the cat was getting closer each passing second.

There had to be a way to control this, to bring some kind of closure to this whole situation.

She flipped over onto her back and stared at the ceiling. She wanted her life back. Without fear.

"Okay, God, if You're real and You care like Kyle says, then show me how to end this. Give me or Kyle or someone a plan or something. And while I'm talking to You…" She shook her head, feeling ridiculous for talking aloud to someone she couldn't see. "Please heal my father."

She lay there for a moment waiting for something to happen, lightning to strike, inspiration to hit. Nothing.

Disappointed, she rose and changed into slacks and a lightweight sweater that Jackie had also brought from Brenda's apartment.

She went downstairs to the living room. Trevor paced in front of the windows like a caged tiger. Jackie sat on the floor with a disassembled gun laid out before her.

"Where's Kyle?" she asked.

"Doing a perimeter sweep," Jackie answered.

Feeling useless and helpless, Brenda decided to go through her files again. She fired up her Heritage Hospital computer and logged in to her account. She down-loaded her email and saw the Evite reminder of the hospital's annual fundraiser.

She was listed as one of the speakers. Kyle had already nixed going, saying it would be too much of a security risk. Her finger hovered over the delete button.

But that was before he'd brought Trevor and Jackie on board.

Besides, these things always had a high number of security personnel because the donor base was some of the city's most prominent and wealthy citizens.

She sighed. But it would be foolish to attend. Why put herself and everyone else at risk?

"That was a heavy sigh," Kyle said, taking a seat in the chair next to her.

His thigh brushed hers, sending awareness of his closeness shooting through her system. His scent, a mixture of musk and man and fresh autumn air, swirled around her head, igniting all her senses and making her frustration even more pronounced because she wanted nothing more than to lean into him and pretend the world didn't exist. But that wasn't possible. And giving in to her yearnings wouldn't accomplish anything. At this point she wasn't sure anything would ever change.

"Yeah, well. This guy is winning," she said, fighting back the burn of tears. "I'm living in fear, trapped inside this place, afraid to go to work, to live my life. How do people live with this kind of constant threat hanging over their life?"

Kyle rubbed her shoulder. "It's natural to feel the way you're feeling. It's never easy. But he hasn't won. I won't let him."

"So we just sit here, day after day, waiting for him to screw up so the police can arrest him. I can't do this anymore." She stared Kyle directly in the eye. "I want my life back."

Kyle slowly nodded. "I want to give it back to you." He ran a hand through his hair and looked at her computer. He leaned forward and pointed at the screen. "And this just might be the way to do it."

A flutter of hope and excitement mixed with anxiety formed a ball in Brenda's tummy. "What are you thinking?"

"If you want to trap a rabid animal, you have to lure it in with bait."

THIRTEEN

On Friday evening, Brenda slipped her feet into a pair of black satin heels. She wasn't used to wearing heels, but they were more comfortable than she remembered. A good thing, because tonight she would be so far out of her comfort zone with everything else going on, and she was glad she wouldn't be complaining about her feet. She was almost ready for the hospital's fall gala. She smoothed a hand down the front of the dress in a lame attempt to settle the nervous flutters in her tummy.

Rather than risk another trip to her apartment, Kyle had insisted she and Jackie pick up dresses at a nearby boutique. Brenda had chosen a basic black, floor-length gown with a boatneck collar and sheer long sleeves. The dress fit like a dream and made her feel svelte and beautiful. She wondered what Kyle would think of the dress.

The minute the thought formed, she realized how much she hoped he liked it—liked her in it.

With shaky hands, she twisted her hair up into a knot, leaving her neck exposed.

A knock sounded on the bedroom door.

Anticipation sent a fresh wave of flutters through her. Kyle? "Come in."

"Almost ready?" Jackie asked as she entered and closed the door behind her.

Disappointment shot through Brenda. "Yes. Almost. That dress is stunning on you."

Jackie twirled. "I feel so young in it."

She'd purchased a stunning silk, pink, off-the-shoulder dress that fell just below her knees. She wore sparkly silver, low-heeled sandals that would allow her to chase bad guys if the need arose. Her blond curls cascaded like a waterfall from a silver clip. Brenda admired the petite woman and was thankful she was here.

With quick steps Jackie crossed to the bed and sat on the edge. She slipped off her shoes and rubbed at her feet. "I've only had these on for five minutes and already my feet hurt," she groused.

"The price for beauty," Brenda commented. A price she usually didn't care to pay. Sure, she had a few pieces of vanity. Her red rubber-soled pumps that she normally wore at work had little bows, but they were still practical. But since Kyle had come into her life, she wanted to look good, to feel pretty.

Jackie's mouth quirked. "We do look great."

Brenda wished she had Jackie's confidence. "I'm nervous," she admitted. Though she wasn't sure if her nerves were more from the dangers ahead or because Kyle would be her escort.

This wasn't a date, she reminded herself. But she wished it were. She wished they were just a normal couple headed to a fancy event where she'd give her speech then they'd leave and head somewhere quiet to have coffee and talk.

But that wasn't the case tonight.

She'd agreed to be bait, to appear in public in hopes her would-be assassin would show himself.

"Kyle made arrangements with Detective Lebowitz for a visible police presence and for undercover cops to pose as part of the waitstaff," Jackie said. "Trevor and I will mingle among the guests. If anyone tries anything, we'll take 'em down." She pumped her fist.

Brenda remembered that Kyle had referred to Jackie as a firecracker. The woman was definitely feisty and fierce. "I wish I was as brave as you."

"I know this has been hard." Jackie pinned her with a compassionate look. "You're doing really well."

Brenda wasn't so sure. She was having a hard time keeping her guard up and not letting the fear overcome her. She could feel the fissures in her composure. "I'm close to cracking."

"You won't crack. You're strong." Jackie slipped her shoes back on. "Besides, Kyle won't let anything happen to you."

"I know he won't." She'd seen him in action, knew what he was capable of. She trusted he'd do everything in his power to protect her.

But would he be able to protect himself, as well? She was afraid for him. She might be the bait, but he wouldn't hesitate to step in front of her and take the hit. The thought of anything happening to him rocked her to her core.

All she could think about was him. So strong. So kind. So handsome. Her heart pounded, an odd mixture of fear and attraction. She was falling for him. Maybe she'd already fallen. That frightened her as much as what might happen tonight.

She wanted the killer found and arrested. But she didn't want Kyle to go away. But that's what would happen once the case was solved and she was no longer in danger.

"If this doesn't end tonight, how much longer can this go on?"

Jackie made a face. "Hard to say. Long enough for you and Kyle to get cozier."

"What? That's ridiculous." A flush started to spread from Brenda's neckline upward while an excited thrill danced down her spine.

"No, it's not." Jackie gave her a knowing look. "You both have it bad. I've seen the way you two look at each other. The way you each anticipate the other's moves and practically finish each other's sentences."

Hoping her rising blush wasn't noticeable, Brenda shook her head and busied her hands by putting on a pair of earrings. Her first line of defense was denial, both to herself and Jackie. "I don't know what you mean."

Jackie's chuckle grated on Brenda's nerves as she fumbled with the earrings.

"There's nothing cozy about being targeted for murder," Brenda said.

"You're right there," Jackie said. "However, I'm not talking about being lax or even relaxed. I'm talking about L-O-V-E."

Brenda stilled. Love?

Her heart pounding in sporadic beats, Brenda turned to face Jackie. She tried to squelch the rising hope. "Look, I know you mean well, but you're way off base. Kyle and I… He's doing a job. I have to trust him. Anything else would be disastrous."

Jackie gave her a searching look. "Why?"

Words tumbled out of Brenda and anxiety swelled in her chest. She locked her fingers together to steady herself. "We have very different lives. We both have demanding careers. He's leaving when this is over. I'm not his type. He likes to play the field. It wouldn't work." *I won't risk my heart again.*

Jackie rose with a shrug. "Sounds like excuses to me." She opened the bedroom door. Then paused to say, "I've known him for several years, and I've never seen him this way with anyone else. He's smitten, even if he doesn't realize it. And I think you are, too, and even if you won't admit it to me, you need to acknowledge it to yourself." Her delicate brows lowered. "And just to set the record straight, Kyle is not a player. He's as solid as they come. Sure he's dated, but he's not a womanizer."

With that Jackie departed, leaving Brenda reeling. She slowly sank onto the bed as she absorbed Jackie's words. Kyle was smitten with her? He wasn't a womanizer?

She was smitten with him?

A laugh escaped. Yes. She was smitten. More than smitten.

She loved Kyle.

The admission welled up from a deep place within that went beyond logic and reason. She loved him.

Joy bubbled, but she tempered it down with reality.

What she'd said to Jackie may have sounded like excuses, but the underlying truth of the reasons remained. And she didn't know how they could change the facts, even if they both wanted to. They lived in different cities. He had a dangerous job that required him to put his life on the line. She was a workaholic with no taste for danger. She couldn't imagine spending the rest of her life constantly worrying that something would happen to him.

Excuses. Jackie's voice rang in Brenda's head.

Maybe. But she was a realist. And a coward. She couldn't put her heart at risk.

She needed to get through this nightmare in one piece.

Anything more was beyond her. When this was over, she'd say goodbye and get on with her life. Without him.

Her heart ached at the thought, but she was determined to stay resolved.

She realized keeping her resolution through the night would be difficult the moment she and Jackie joined Kyle and Trevor, both dressed to impress in traditional black tuxedos and stunningly handsome.

Her gaze was drawn straight to Kyle's. His blue eyes widened, and an appreciative grin lit up his face. Her insides clenched.

"You're beautiful," he said with something like awe in his tone.

"So are you," she said, liking the way his tux fit across his broad shoulders. He'd combed his hair into submission away from his face, emphasizing the strong line of his jaw and chiseled cheekbones. She wanted to kiss every angle and plane of his face. She tightened her hold on her evening bag.

"Come on, folks." Trevor, looking like a James Bond candidate, picked up the duffel bag with their weapons. "Time to get this show going."

They arrived at the Grand Hotel ten minutes later. They were escorted to the Grand Ballroom. The vast space was set up with white linen-covered tables, a stage and podium at one end and fresh-cut flowers everywhere. Even the balconies were decorated with ivy intertwined through the railings. Huge gilded baskets filled to the brim with exotic blooms hung from the ceiling on clear string, making them appear as if they were floating in the air.

These events always were torture for Brenda. But

tonight, her anxiety level went through the roof. Making small talk was difficult for her. Add in a potential murderer, and she was a bundle of nerves. However, she soon discovered that Kyle was a master at carrying the conversation as he moved her through the crowd, stopping to say hello and introduce themselves to complete strangers. Brenda caught sight of Trevor near the main entrance. He seemed to be scrutinizing those entering the ballroom. Jackie floated about the room, mingling sporadically like a pink pixie. Brenda doubted anyone realized the diminutive operative was scoping out possible bad guys.

By the time Kyle led Brenda to a table near the front of the room, Brenda's shoulder muscles screamed with tension. With every brush of Kyle's arm against hers, every time he placed his hand to the small of her back, all her nerve endings tingled, making it hard to concentrate on anything other than him.

Brenda and Kyle were seated with some very wealthy patrons of the hospital. The woman on Brenda's left wanted to talk health-care reform, a subject Brenda had plenty to say on. She was thankfully able to shift her focus away from her troubles for a few moments.

The emcee approached the microphone on the podium. "Thank you, ladies and gentlemen, for joining us at our tenth annual fall fundraising gala. We have several guests here tonight, including two of Heritage Hospital's finest physicians. They will speak later this evening. But first we have a special treat for you tonight. Please give a big welcome to country-music star R. C. Spinoza."

Kyle leaned over to whisper in her ear, "You doing okay?"

His breath tickled her neck and sent delicious shivers sliding over her. She leaned closer to whisper back, "With you here I am."

He drew back to hold her gaze. "Good to know."

Pulse skittering, Brenda was glad they weren't alone, because the longing to explore just what the look in his eyes meant squeezed her in a tight grip. A waiter stepped between them to refill her water glass. The buzz and chatter of a full banquet room rose. She took a cooling sip of water and focused on making polite conversation with the others at the table.

An hour later, a prickling of unease made Brenda stiffen. The waiter hovered near her elbow. She drew back slightly to look at him. He met her gaze. Cold gray eyes bore into her. His face looked familiar. Bold features, a broad forehead and close-cropped hair. Brenda knew she'd seen the man before. His image bounced through her memories but never settled.

"Coffee?" he asked.

With the beat of her heart sounding in her head in time to the country tune being sung at the front of the room, she shook her head. He moved on to the next table.

Spooked, she tried to remember where she'd seen the guy.

Kyle laid a hand on her arm. "Everything okay?"

"I thought I recognized one of the waitstaff," she whispered.

"Which one?"

Her gaze sought the waiter with the cold gray eyes, but she didn't see him. "Close-cropped dark hair. Gray eyes. Not as tall as you." She shook her head, frustrated. "There's too many of them. I can't pick him out."

Kyle stood and laid a hand on her shoulder. "I'll be right back. You stay put."

A flutter of panic hit her tummy. "Where are you going?"

"To talk to Lebowitz. Have him find the guy you saw. Half of the waiters are Chicago P.D., but the others…"

…could be the one who wanted her dead. Did she recognize the man because he was a police officer?

Watching Kyle weave his way through the crush of tables, she tested that thought, but it didn't jell in her mind. She tuned out the room and searched her brain. Where had she seen that man? The hospital? The clinic?

He'd been dressed differently, though. Not in the white shirt and black slacks of the waitstaff. No, she could almost picture him in work boots and a plaid shirt.

Something clicked, and suddenly she knew why he looked familiar.

She'd seen him only once. Two years ago at the downtown clinic. He was a construction worker, if she remembered correctly.

He and his wife had brought in their son, who had presented with a splenic rupture. From a fall off his bike, the mother, a small, wispy woman with a soft voice, had said.

The spleen was the most frequent organ to be damaged in blunt-trauma injury involving the abdomen. A fall off a bike, catching a handlebar in the stomach region, could have explained the injury. However, during the surgery to remove the damaged organ, Brenda had noticed other bruises not consistent with a fall.

While the boy recovered, Brenda had followed protocol and informed child protective services. Then she'd moved on to another patient.

She'd never seen the family again. Never knew what happened to the boy or his parents. She'd done her job and left CPS to do theirs.

Could he be the man who wanted her dead?

"Brenda?"

Kyle's touch on her arm jolted her out of her thoughts. She turned and looked into his concerned blue eyes. He slipped back into his seat. "Did you find the waiter?"

"No," he said. "And no one remembers seeing anyone like you described. But Lebowitz has his men searching. I'm not going to let anyone get near you."

She clutched his arm. "I remembered where I'd seen him. He's the father of a patient I had a few years ago. He abused his son. I reported him."

Tension came off Kyle in waves. He rose. "We're leaving."

She moved to follow just as the emcee announced her name.

"They just introduced you," he said, his gaze narrowing. "Are you okay?"

She heard the polite applause, felt the expectant stares and forced herself to function. She was supposed to give a speech, but her mind was a complete blank.

Panic battered at her. "I have to give my speech." Mustering all her reserves, she forced the panic aside and fought for her control. "The only way to catch him is if he tries something. The only way that will happen is if I go up there."

Kyle shook his head and tugged at her to follow him. "No."

She didn't move. "You'll be with me. Nothing will happen. You'll make sure nothing happens to me."

Praying the words of her speech would come, she headed toward the front of the ballroom. Kyle let out a frustrated growl and followed with his hand at her back. Her gaze scanned the sea of bodies, looking for that man. She didn't see him. It had to be coincidence that he'd be a waiter here tonight. Didn't it?

Kyle made her pause before stepping onto the platform while he consulted with Detective Lebowitz. Several of the waitstaff had formed a barrier of sorts around the stage. These were Chicago police officers disguised as waiters. She saw Jackie standing off to the left and Trevor to the right. Both appeared to be alert and ready for action. Seeing them bolstered her flagging courage.

"Stay behind the podium," Kyle whispered in her ear. "If I say 'duck,' you duck."

A boulder of fear pressed on her chest. So much for her courage. She drew in air and slowly let it out, trying to calm her nerves. At Kyle's nod, she approached the podium. The glare of floodlights shining in her face made everyone in the room blur. She glanced at Kyle. He stood onstage within reach if she needed him. Drawing strength from his presence, she began her speech.

Kyle hated how exposed and vulnerable Brenda was on the platform, standing behind a thin wood podium. Her strong voice filled the room as she spoke about the need for funds to advance the technology of Heritage Hospital's surgical department.

Every precaution had been taken. He was in constant communication with Trevor and Jackie through their earpieces. They were keeping a close eye on the tables and the waitstaff. Lebowitz had officers stationed throughout the ballroom. Kyle had informed the detective of the suspicious waiter. He was looking for someone who matched the description Brenda gave. If Brenda's assassin tried anything, he'd go down quickly.

Still, Kyle knew how quickly and easily even the best-laid strategies could be derailed.

Always plan for the unexpected, his CO used to say.

Lots harder to do in practice than theory. He scanned the balconies, looking for anything out of place, but the lights had been dimmed. He could make out only the silhouettes of diners listening with rapt attention.

A creaking noise, barely audible above Brenda's voice, shot a spike of adrenaline through his system. He moved closer, trying to discern where the noise originated.

Brenda ended her speech. The crowd erupted in applause. Just as she turned to leave the platform, Kyle heard the snap, felt the swoosh of air as the hanging basket over Brenda's head came hurtling down. A collective gasp rippled through the room. Someone screamed. Kyle sprang forward, snagging Brenda by the waist and diving off the platform, taking her with him. He rolled as they landed so that he took the brunt of the fall. Pain reverberated where his shoulder and hip connected with the floor. The basket crashed onto the platform, pulverizing the podium.

Three loud bangs sent a deafening shock wave through the room as an intense flash of light lit up the room. The ballroom broke out in pandemonium.

Flash bombs.

Kyle clutched Brenda against his chest, glad they were low enough that the blinding light hadn't affected his vision. The flash of light undoubtedly momentarily blinded everyone else in the room. His ears, however, rang from the explosion.

"Are you hurt?" he yelled over the din of chaos.

She clung to him. "No."

Relieved she was unharmed, he got his feet under him and helped her to stand. He had to get her to safety. Where were Trevor and Jackie?

He couldn't see them in the crush of people pushing toward the exits. Leading with his shoulder, he plowed a path through the crowd and out the door.

Lebowitz met them outside the ballroom.

"This way," he shouted, directing them toward a closed door, marked Employees Only.

The door led to a dark cement corridor.

"This is the employee entrance," Lebowitz explained. "It comes out by the valet parking lot. I'll make sure no one follows you."

Kyle kept Brenda close as they ran. They heard Lebowitz yell, "Stop. Police."

Then gunfire.

The sound of people running toward them spurred Kyle to move faster. Someone fired at them. Bullets ricocheted off the cement walls. Kyle grabbed for his weapon and reached back to return fire.

They came to the end of the tunnel.

Brenda tried the door. "No!" She pounded on the locked door.

Frantic, Kyle pulled her out of the way and gave the door a hard kick, hoping to bust the lock. It wouldn't budge.

Four men crowded into the corridor behind them and blocked the only escape.

They were trapped. There was nowhere to go. Nowhere to hide.

His heart dropped. Fear tightened a noose around his neck. He pushed Brenda behind him to shield her.

"Kyle?"

Brenda's panicked whisper stabbed at the very core of his being. In the space of a heartbeat, he realized the undeniable and dreadful fact that he'd failed to protect an amazing, wonderful woman who'd worked her way into the very fiber of his being.

Please, Lord, save the woman I love.

Brenda fisted her hand in the back of Kyle's tux jacket. Four men with big guns stared at them. They were all dressed as waitstaff. One of the men stepped forward, the glow of the single overhead light revealing his face.

The man she'd recognized earlier.

"You!" Kyle said.

The man smiled smugly. "Me. Now drop your weapon."

Brenda didn't understand. How did Kyle know this man?

Kyle held up his hands as he bent to lay his gun on the floor. "What is this about?"

The man ignored his question to focus those cruel gray eyes on Brenda. She shuddered and moved closer to Kyle.

"Finally," their attacker said. "You are one tough woman to kill."

She flinched as if he'd struck her.

"Who are you?" Kyle demanded.

"Ask her," the man said with a sneer. "Ask her if she remembers ruining my life."

Brenda gaped. Anger burst through the fear. "You beat your son."

"So you say," the man snapped.

"I remember a little boy who needed his spleen removed because you'd punched him," she shot back. "That was what had actually happened, right? Not some biking accident, like you and your wife claimed."

"You had no right to call the cops," he said. "I went to jail because of you, and now you're gonna pay."

He raised his gun.

Realizing that to get to her he'd have to shoot Kyle first, Brenda stepped out from behind Kyle. Kyle tried to pull her back. She refused. If she was going to die, it wouldn't be cowering behind the man she loved. "He has nothing to do with this. Let him go."

"And let him blab to the police," the man scoffed. "No way. You both have to die." He pulled the trigger.

Kyle's strong arms wrapped around her and yanked her to the floor.

A cacophony of noise bounced off the concrete walls and echoed in her brain, rattling her mind.

She flinched, closing her eyes tight. *Dear Lord, help!*

Silence filled the corridor.

Brenda didn't feel any pain, only Kyle's arms holding her safely against his body. She lifted her head and whipped her gaze around. The gunmen lay on the ground, bleeding from leg and shoulder wounds. The man who'd tried to kill Brenda was hunched over on the ground, a bullet wound in his upper back. Behind them stood Trevor and Jackie, their guns still raised.

For a shocked moment, Brenda couldn't believe they'd been spared. Then she looked at Kyle. His eyes were closed, his complexion white. A crimson-red stain spread across the stark white of his dress shirt. He'd been shot.

Terror unlike she'd ever known choked her. "Kyle!"

She scrambled out of his arms to check his pulse. Weak, but there. She pressed her hands over the wound to stem the flow of blood. "Call 911!"

Blood seeped through her fingers. Kyle's blood. His

life was ebbing out of him and she couldn't stop it. Tears fell and a sob broke through.

Pain jolted Kyle awake.

Brenda!

He tried to sit up, but gentle hands held him down.

"Shh," a familiar and beloved voice said. Brenda. "Take it easy. You're safe."

Prying his eyelids open by sheer force of will, he winced as daylight stung his eyes. Then he saw her face.

Brenda. Alive and well. Tears blurred his vision. He blinked them back. She looked so much as she had that first day. Her hair pulled back in a tight bun. Dark clothes beneath her lab coat. He couldn't see if she had on the red pumps or not. He really liked those red shoes.

Just as he loved this beautiful, tough, amazing woman. His heart hammered in his chest.

God had given them a chance at a future. Together. He wanted to shout it out loud. He wanted to take her into his arms and hold her tight. He lifted his hand, but the movement sent a fire trail of pain shooting through him.

"How… What happened?" he asked, his voice coming out hoarse. He remembered seeing Trevor and Jackie advancing. Remembered the sound of gunfire. The searing pain.

"You were shot in the shoulder." She gave a wry twist to her lips. "And in the chest, but the body armor stopped that bullet from piercing your heart."

"Praise God for small favors."

"Here, try to drink some water." She cradled his hand and lifted a cup to his lips. He sipped the cool liquid.

When he'd had his fill, he asked, "You? You're okay?"

A tender smile curved her lips. "Yes. You saved me yet again."

"Doing my job," he quipped.

She studied him for a moment. "Yes, well, your job is over. Simon Leto, the man who wanted to kill me, is in jail, and so are his cohorts."

"He was the one who tried to deliver flowers to your apartment that first day," he said.

"I wondered how you knew him."

"Lebowitz?"

"He was shot in the abdomen. Thankfully no vital organs were hit. He's recovering nicely, as well," she said.

"Good." He was relieved to know the detective hadn't died. "Trevor and Jackie?"

"They're out in the waiting room." She gave him a stiff smile. "I'll go get them for you."

He snagged her wrist before she could move away. "I'd rather you didn't."

She stared at him. "Why?"

"Because I'd rather you stayed here with me."

"You don't need me," she said, her expression closed off. "Your vitals look good."

But he did need her. And he was going to do everything in his power to make her see that. He shook his head. "My heart hurts."

Concern darkened her eyes. "I can get you some more pain medication."

"Meds won't help what I've got," he said. He searched her face, memorizing the curve of her cheek, the bow of her lips. He loved this woman with his whole being. He wasn't sure how she felt, but facing his own mortality and dealing with the possibility of losing Brenda had made him realize he wasn't going to waste any time wondering and speculating. He had to tell her how he felt, and he'd do whatever it took to ensure their future was spent together.

He stroked the soft skin of her wrist where her pulse beat. "I love you."

Her pulse jumped beneath his touch. Her eyes grew wide. "You do?"

"I do." He drew in a bracing breath. "I've spent my whole life pushing people away. Afraid to let myself love. Telling myself it was better to be free than settled down. I told myself a lot things that were just excuses to keep people at arm's length. I thought life would be easier without any ties. But I was wrong. I want to be settled down. I want to be tied to someone. I want to be tied to you." He was baring his soul, and it was as scary as diving out the back of air transport at ten thousand feet and his parachute failing. He swallowed and forced himself to continue. "I hope…I pray that you… might feel something for me?"

Disbelief gave way to joy as a smile that could light up the whole city spread across her face. "Oh, yes. I feel something, all right. I've been fighting it from the day you walked into Dr. Landsem's office. I thought you were everything I'm not. Brave, honorable and kind."

"But you are those things," he protested.

She shook her head. "No. I was afraid of being hurt. I'd closed myself off to everyone and everything. I wasn't really living, only existing. But then you came along and made me feel. Made me want to be a better person. You taught me about faith." She smiled softly. "I admire your faith. I admire you." She cupped his face with her hands. "I love you."

Elation filled him. "Then kiss me."

"My pleasure," she said and dipped her head.

Her lips were tender and sweet, and when she lifted her head, he groaned. "No, don't stop."

The look of uncertainty in her eyes sobered him. "Brenda?"

"How will we do this, Kyle? Your life is in Boston. Mine is here."

He wasn't going to let her push him away. He tugged her closer. "Logistics."

Her mouth curved in a wry smile. "Excuses."

They were on the same page. Good. "I'm sure my boss wouldn't mind if I open an office here. Or maybe the Chicago P.D. would have room for a frogman."

Tears welled in her eyes. "You'd do that? You'd move here? For me?"

He nodded. "But only if you'll kiss me again."

"Every day for the rest of our lives," she said and pressed her lips to his.

* * * * *

Dear Reader,

Thank you for spending time with Brenda and Kyle. This is the third book in the Protection Specialists miniseries. Kyle Martin appeared in the first two books, *The Innocent Witness* (July 2011) and *The Secret Heiress* (January 2012), as well as a 2009 online read for Harlequin titled *Yuletide Peril.* Though he was a secondary character, there was something about him that drew me in and made me want to write his romance. He was brash and irreverent and reminded me a lot of my own hero, my husband.

It took me a while to find the right heroine for Kyle. I wanted someone he'd have to work hard to impress, someone he'd want to understand in order to have a happily-ever-after. And of course there had to be a suspense plot to hang their romance on. I started playing with ideas, and Dr. Brenda Storm was created. She was emotionally closed off but didn't realize she was. She was ambitious and determined but also a bit socially unaware. She seemed the perfect flip side of Kyle. When I decided to put her life in danger, I knew Kyle had to protect her, but I also knew Brenda would chafe at having protection, which made the sparks fly as they learned to appreciate their differences and their similarities in order to stay alive and fall in love. I hope you found their story enjoyable.

The fourth installment of the Protection Specialists will be out in early 2013. Also in May 2013, I have a continuity book coming out that will feature the cutest member of the Texas K-9 unit—a drug-sniffing beagle named Sherlock and his handsome handler, Parker Adams.

Until next time, may God keep you in His care,

Terri Reed

Questions for Discussion

1. What made you pick up this book to read? In what ways did the cover capture your attention? Can you discuss how the back-cover blurb intrigued you? In what ways did this book live up to your expectations?

2. In what ways were Brenda and Kyle realistic characters? What stands out most vividly to you about each character?

3. How did the romance build believably? Can you talk about the traits that each character discovered in each other? Are these traits you see in your significant relationships?

4. How did the suspense build? Did you notice clues to the villain?

5. What about the setting was clear and appealing?

6. Dr. Brenda Storm believed she had to be perfect because that was what was expected of her. Can you talk about what expectations you feel? Where are those expectations coming from?

7. Kyle's faith was strong in the story. Brenda questioned God and faith. Where do you stand in your faith? Can you talk about how you came to know the Lord? Was there someone instrumental in helping you to develop your faith?

8. Brenda closed herself off emotionally after a failed romance. Discuss an emotional wound that you struggled to overcome. How did you overcome the hurt?

9. Kyle felt guilty for the abuse his sister suffered. What, if anything, could he have done to help her?

10. As a doctor, Brenda was obligated to report any suspicion of abuse to a patient who is a minor. I believe each of us should report any suspicion of abuse whether we're a doctor or teacher. Discuss ways we all can help protect children. Have you ever suspected someone was being abused? What did you do?

11. What does the verse at the beginning of the book mean to you?

12. Brenda drew upon her early Sunday-school teachings in order to find it within herself to reach out to God. What seeds of faith were planted early in your life? Can you share a story from your childhood where faith played an important role?

13. How did the author's use of language/writing style make this an enjoyable read?

14. Discuss whether you would or would not read more from this author. What books by this author have you read?

15. What will be your most vivid memories of this book? What lessons about life, love and faith did you learn from this story?

REQUEST YOUR FREE BOOKS!

2 FREE RIVETING INSPIRATIONAL NOVELS
PLUS 2 FREE MYSTERY GIFTS

Love Inspired
SUSPENSE

YES! Please send me 2 FREE Love Inspired® Suspense novels and my 2 FREE mystery gifts (gifts are worth about $10). After receiving them, if I don't wish to receive any more books, I can return the shipping statement marked "cancel". If I don't cancel, I will receive 4 brand-new novels every month and be billed just $4.49 per book in the U.S. or $4.99 per book in Canada. That's a saving of at least 22% off the cover price. It's quite a bargain! Shipping and handling is just 50¢ per book in the U.S. and 75¢ per book in Canada.* I understand that accepting the 2 free books and gifts places me under no obligation to buy anything. I can always return a shipment and cancel at any time. Even if I never buy another book, the two free books and gifts are mine to keep forever.

123/323 IDN FEHR

Name	(PLEASE PRINT)	
Address		Apt. #
City	State/Prov.	Zip/Postal Code

Signature (if under 18, a parent or guardian must sign)

Mail to the **Reader Service:**
IN U.S.A.: P.O. Box 1867, Buffalo, NY 14240-1867
IN CANADA: P.O. Box 609, Fort Erie, Ontario L2A 5X3

Not valid for current subscribers to Love Inspired Suspense books.

**Are you a subscriber to Love Inspired Suspense
and want to receive the larger-print edition?
Call 1-800-873-8635 or visit www.ReaderService.com.**

* Terms and prices subject to change without notice. Prices do not include applicable taxes. Sales tax applicable in N.Y. Canadian residents will be charged applicable taxes. Offer not valid in Quebec. This offer is limited to one order per household. All orders subject to credit approval. Credit or debit balances in a customer's account(s) may be offset by any other outstanding balance owed by or to the customer. Please allow 4 to 6 weeks for delivery. Offer available while quantities last.

Your Privacy—The Reader Service is committed to protecting your privacy. Our Privacy Policy is available online at www.ReaderService.com or upon request from the Reader Service.

We make a portion of our mailing list available to reputable third parties that offer products we believe may interest you. If you prefer that we not exchange your name with third parties, or if you wish to clarify or modify your communication preferences, please visit us at www.ReaderService.com/consumerschoice or write to us at Reader Service Preference Service, P.O. Box 9062, Buffalo, NY 14269. Include your complete name and address.

LISUS11B

celebrating 15 YEARS

SUSPENSE

RIVETING INSPIRATIONAL ROMANCE

ASSIGNMENT: BLACKMAIL

Stephanie Gage's father has been kidnapped—by a dangerous man who wants to make a trade. Her beloved dad for a multimillion-dollar family heirloom that's gone missing. To track it down, she must rely on demolitions expert Tate Fuego— the man who broke her heart years ago. Stephanie knows that Tate's reasons for helping have nothing to do with her. But trusting Tate is all that stands between Stephanie and a madman's ultimate revenge.

Will Stephanie and Tate be able to find
the missing heirloom in time?

Find out in

DANGEROUS MELODY

by

DANA MENTINK

TREASURE SEEKERS

**Available
November 2012**

www.LoveInspiredBooks.com

—TEXAS TWINS—

Follow the adventure of two sets of twins who are torn
apart by family secrets and learn to find their way home.

Her Surprise Sister by Marta Perry
July 2012

Mirror Image Bride by Barbara McMahon
August 2012

Carbon Copy Cowboy by Arlene James
September 2012

Look-Alike Lawman by Glynna Kaye
October 2012

The Soldier's Newfound Family
by Kathryn Springer
November 2012

Reunited for the Holidays
by Jillian Hart
December 2012

*Available wherever
books are sold.*

www.LoveInspiredBooks.com

LICONT0912